# THE LAND I DREAM OF

Manisha Sobhrajani has been a journalist and researcher. A casual recreational trip to Kashmir became a ten-year-long association with its people, especially the women. She now spends her days as a full-time volunteer with the Samarpan Foundation in the Sunderbans, West Bengal. *The Land I Dream of* is her first book.

# The Land I Dream of

*The Story of Kashmir's Women*

Manisha Sobhrajani

hachette INDIA

First published in 2014 by Hachette India
(Registered name: Hachette Book Publishing India Pvt. Ltd)
An Hachette UK company
www.hachetteindia.com

SRD



ISBN 978-93-5009-222-4

Hachette Book Publishing India Pvt. Ltd
4th/5th Floors, Corporate Centre,
Sector 44, Gurgaon 122003, India

Typeset in Arno Pro 12/15
by InoSoft Systems, Noida
Printed and bound in India by Manipal Technologies Limited, Manipal

FSC www.fsc.org
MIX
Paper | Supporting responsible forestry
FSC™ C043100

*Because of Patrick*

*and*

*For Mallika and Hitesh*

# Contents

# Introduction

*Resilience: to stand in the path of lightning.*
*Resilience: to walk when darkness falls at noon.*
*Resilience: to grind yourself fine in the turning mill.*
*Resilience will come to you.*[1]

This *vakh,* or verse, by Kashmir's very own Lal Ded best describes the people of Jammu and Kashmir. Living amidst the chaos, confusion, turmoil and trauma of a prolonged conflict, the people have had no choice but to endure what came their way. All the discussions have, however, centred around how the men have endured the long conflict, and it is rare to come across a woman's account of the war. Kashmiri women – mothers, wives, sisters and daughters – have spent the better part of their lives negotiating space for their menfolk and living through the conflict in their own ways. For Kashmiri women, it has become a way of life to take up the issue of missing sons and husbands; some of them have fought in the conflict, participated in it wilfully or hid militants at their homes. Yet, it is women whose viewpoint has been sidelined, ignored, even suppressed.

I grew up with a stereotypical notion of Kashmiri women: in my teenage head, they were extremely pretty, and their fair and delicate skin was prone to damage at the slightest touch. My notions were confirmed when Sharmila Tagore immortalized the quintessential *Kashmir ki kali* in a Bollywood film of the same name. This bubble burst on my very first trip to the valley, in 2003. Kashmiri women are very pretty, no doubt. But their fair and delicate skin has also been prone to damage, not just by a mere touch, but as a result of the tug of war between India and Pakistan over their land. For the women of Kashmir, the impact of this political tragedy has been doubly fatal; they have not just borne the wrath of the conflict, but they have also been treated as objects of use and amusement, both by militants as well as by Indian security forces. Azaadi (freedom) – both personal as well as political – has remained a distant dream.

The state of J&K has been a bone of contention between India and Pakistan for more than six decades now. The two nations have fought four wars – in 1947, 1965, 1971 and 1999 – and have been very close to a war-like situation twice – in 2002, after the attack on the Indian Parliament, and in 2008, after the terror attacks in Mumbai. The former princely state (pre-1947) is now divided into three parts: Indian-administered Kashmir (IAK), Pakistan-administered Kashmir (PAK), and the Northern Areas, which are also controlled by Pakistan.[2] A sizeable chunk of the state – Aksai Chin and Shaksgam valley – was ceded by Pakistan to China.[3]

Political troubles in Kashmir can be traced back to the eighth century, when Kashmir grew as a colonial power under the Karkota dynasty. The Karkota King Lalitaditya Muktapida brought the kingdoms of Magadha, Kamarupa, Gauda and Kalinga under his empire, but after his death, the reins was taken over by the Utpala dynasty. A politically unstable Kashmir of the tenth century made its royal guards – the Tantrins – very influential, and under them, chaos prevailed. Queen Didda took over the rule of Kashmir under extremely turbulent times, in the second half of the tenth century, only to give way to the Lohara dynasty. Oppression of the masses and the rise of feudalism paved the way for foreign invasions of Kashmir, including two failed attempts by Mahmud of Ghazni in the eleventh century. A Turkish-Mongol chief, followed by a Tibetan-Buddhist refugee, who converted to Islam, created further mayhem. It was in the fourteenth century that Islam finally became the dominant religion in Kashmir.

For the purposes of this book, I will dwell only on its modern history, beginning in 1946, which is imperative to understanding the present conflict. Let us first take a look at the myths around how Kashmir was created.

In his book *Kashmir: Behind the Vale* (Roli Books, 2002), journalist and author M.J. Akbar says, 'At the beginning of Kalpa, or Creation, the valley was a lake hundreds of feet deep, called the Sati Saras, or the Lake of Sati, consort of Kashmir's preferred lord, Shiva. In this lake lived the demon Jalodbhav or the One Born in Water, who terrorized the Nagas, snakes who guarded the waters (the word is still used to name places, like Anantnag).'[4] The Nagas did not appear as snakes; they guarded the waters either as clouds, hailstorm or other natural phenomenon. Jalodbhav's tyranny was unacceptable to the Nagas, but there was little that they could do. When the sage Kashyapa, said to be the father of the Nagas, found out, he was livid. Raging with anger, he visited Brahma the Creator and requested him to intervene. Brahma, and the other gods who joined him to end Jalodbhav's brutal oppression, devised a plan. They had to keep in mind that Jalodbhav could not be harmed as long as he remained in water. While all the gods took up positions on the various mountain peaks surrounding the Sati Saras lake, Lord Vishnu requested his brother Balabhadra to pierce the mountains so that the waters of the lake could drain out. Balabhadra chose Baramullah as the exit point, and as the waters drained, Vishnu engaged Jalodbhav in battle, and killed him. Kashyapa was indebted to the gods, and so pleased was he that he decided to settle in the dry valley, which was then named after him: Kashmir. The gods, too, were so mesmerized by the beauty of this land that they, along with various goddesses, also settled here.

Perhaps this myth is the starting point for the belief among the people of this land, who are very clear their identity is entirely different from the lesser mortals of the planes. It could also be because the people here are as close to nature as anyone can be, considering that they are literally cut off from the rest of the world for six months during winter, when the only reality of life is snow, and more snow. Perhaps this is nature's way of protecting this paradise on earth. All its main passes – Zojila and Burzil in the north-east, Tosamaidan in the Pir Panjal, Banihal, and the Jehlum valley route via Uri – are guarded by impenetrable snow for most months of the year.

This has ensured that the melting pot of Kashmiri art, culture, tradition, heritage, food, clothing, etc. is barely influenced by the outside world. It is its own, personalized amalgam, a way of life, lovingly and spiritually referred to as 'Kashmiriyat'. Prof. Afaq Aziz Kashmiri explained what Kashmiriyat meant in the most simplified terms: 'Kashmir and its people welcome anyone and everyone who comes here.' I couldn't agree more. I experienced it for myself every day in the ten years I spent in this land, a land that adopted me whole-heartedly, without judging me. In later pages in this book, I have attempted to explain this unique concept in my own words, in a way that I have understood it.

However, once this inaccessible land does get accessed by 'trouble', as has been the case particularly since 1989, it is tough to get rid of it. The same invincible mountains, which guard the valley so ferociously from the enemy, isolate the land in a manner that outside help cannot reach easily, and even when it does, without being connected to the rest of the world, it is tough to make a difference. In this lies the crux of the prolonged Kashmir conflict; the fact that it has taken forever for the outside world to reach out to Kashmir, and even when it has, it has made little difference – in terms of ideas and influences, stocks and supplies, ideologies and interventions, and empathy and care.

The mythical origins of the land and the inaccessibility factor – nature having played a major role in both cases – and the spiritual element of Kashmiriyat made Kashmir a desirable land, much coveted by many. Once this land of myths, legends, fantasies, mysticism and divine intervention finally came into existence, it became the envy of many a historical rulers, and was extremely sought after. The most influencing aspect of Kashmir's history has perhaps been the stimulus provided by the advent of Buddhism. Again, in the words of M.J. Akbar, 'Asoka the Great's soldiers brought Kashmir into the Mauryan empire, and he founded the capital, Srinagar; but the spiritual merit of the emperor's Buddhist missionaries had more impact. The Hindu valley, said by antiquity to have been settled by the sage Kashyapa, devotee of the Lord Shiva, took to Buddhism. Kanishka, the first Indian emperor of Turkish descent, held the Third Great Council of Buddhism in Kashmir. The land accepted the sword, but bowed to faith.'[5] Kashmir remained a Buddhist land until Islam took over. Yet, a lot of Buddhist identities and cultures remain despite the change in religion.

Meanwhile, there was this great wave of faith, enormously spiritual in nature, spreading all across India like a raging fire. Spiritual masters, saints, peers, dervishes and fakirs were feeding this insatiable fire with the fuel of the Bhakti movement. Kashmir, too, got engulfed and completely consumed in this fire.

Take Padmavati for example: born an ordinary mortal in Pandrethan into an ordinary family, she went through the rituals of a very ordinary existence – early marriage in Pampore, and the affairs of an everyday, normal life. Had it not been for a vicious mother-in-law and brutal husband who tormented and tortured her no end, Padmavati would have probably died an ordinary death as well. Her 'fault' was her deep inclination towards a spiritual self, which took precedence over everything else. The ordinary mortal chose to step out of her ordinary existence and went into deep meditation, and came out of it to live an extraordinary life of spirituality. Known by many names – Lalla Arifa, Lalleshwari, Lal Ded – this mystic was single-handedly responsible for writing many of the proverbs and idioms used in the Kashmiri language even today. Displaying immense passion towards the worship of the Divine, Lalla shunned rituals and idol worship practised by priests and mullahs. She challenged them with faith, and her *vakhs*. It is said that she roamed around naked, possessed no material belongings, and instead of renouncing the world, went looking for and awakening the simplicity and goodness in every human heart.

Married at the age of twelve, it is said that Lalla left her marital home at the age of twenty-six to follow the callings of her soul. She asked the Shaivite saint Siddha Srikantha to be her guru, who agreed to guide her along a path of spiritual learning and realization. However, if domestic life was tough, leading a spiritual path as a woman was far tougher. One, it was unchartered territory for women at the time; two, it meant not just renouncing the world and all its material associations, but also renouncing, losing and surrendering one's own self to the Divine, and allowing the Universe to take over and guide one along a pre-destined path.

*They lash me with insults, serenade me with curses.*
*Their barking means nothing to me.*
*Even if they came with soul-flowers to offer,*
*I couldn't care less. Untouched, I move on.*[6]

As long as Lalla was under the tutelage of her guru, she was secure. Once she ventured into the world on her own, not only did she receive criticism, she also had to bear humiliation, particularly because she challenged the existing norms of society as far as devotion and worship were concerned. Lalla, in her own special way, brought the flames of the Bhakti movement to Kashmir. Not only are her *vakhs* splendid examples of opposition to religious orthodoxy and radical worship in simple, everyday language, but her choices also paved the way for future Bhakti women-saints like Mirabai. Naturally, her chosen path was riddled with obstacles, and one on which she walked alone:

*Let them hurl a thousand curses at me,*
*pain finds no purchase in my heart.*
*I belong to Shiva. Can a scatter of ashes*
*ruin a mirror? It gleams.*[7]

Lal Ded's *vakhs* are a mix of Sufism, Shaivism, Islam, Tantra, Buddhism, philosophy and mysticism. Poet and cultural theorist Ranjit Hoskote aptly describes Lalla's *vakhs* thus:[8]

> '...they shuttle between the vulnerability of doubt and the assurance of an insight gained through resilience and reflection. These poems are as likely to demand that the Divine reveal Itself, as to complain of Its bewildering and protean ubiquity. They prize clarity of self-knowledge above both the ritualistic's mastery of observances and the ascetic's professional athleticism. If they scoff at the

scholar who substitutes experience with scripture and the priest who cages his God in a routine of prayers, they also reject the renouncer's austere mortification of the body. Across the expanse of her poetry, the author whose signature these poems carry evolves from a wanderer, uncertain of herself and looking for anchorage in a potentially hostile landscape, into a questor who has found belonging beneath a sky that is continuous with her mind.

*Wear the robe of wisdom,*
*brand Lalla's words on your heart,*
*lose yourself in the soul's light,*
*you too shall be free.'*[9]

Lal Ded's name is synonymous with Kashmir today, and her *vakhs* are an undisputable part of Kashmiri literature. In fact, her *vakhs* established Kashmiri as a modern-day language. However, it is not as simple as it sounds. There is no documentation that can ascertain her birth and death. She is known to have lived in Kashmir in the twelfth or thirteenth century, but beyond that, very little is known of her except from her verses. She belongs as much to the Hindus, who refer to her as Lalleshwari or Lalla Yogini, as she does to the Muslims, to whom she is Lalla Arifa. She is fondly and simply referred to as Lalla, or Lal Ded, meaning Grandmother Lal. All these names are an indication of the love with which Kashmiris, both Hindus and Muslims, revere their first woman mystic saint.

The most beloved of Kashmiri Sufi saints, Sheikh Nuruddin,

was not just Lal Ded's successor; according to legend, she also suckled him at her breast. M.J. Akbar, again in *Kashmir: Behind the Vale,* narrates the story of Nuruddin Rishi's birth. Salar, his father, originally from Kishtwar, found in Yasman Rishi his guru, and respite from the life of a wanderer. Salar converted to Islam, and took on the name of Salar-ud-Din. While Salar was wandering aimlessly, a battle was taking place at Duderkot. The only survivor of the battle, a girl named Sadra, was adopted by a chowkidar. Eventually, the chowkidar died, leaving Sadra orphaned once again. Sadra, too, like Salar, found refuge and protection with Yasman Rishi, who got the two married. After marriage, they settled in the village of Khai Jogipura.

Salar took on the role of chowkidar, in his father-in-law's place. One night, while doing the rounds of his neighbourhood, he overheard a conversation between a sadhu and his wife. While studying the stars, as was his want, the sadhu predicted that a bouquet of roses would appear by the water spring of Khai Jogipura, just before dawn. Any woman who inhaled the fragrance of those roses would give birth to a noble saint whose fame would reach far and wide.

Salar immediately went home to fetch his wife, and they anxiously waited by the spring. Sure enough, the roses appeared at the brink of dawn. Sadra inhaled their fragrance; nine months later, Nuruddin Rishi was born. It is said that for three days, the newborn refrained from suckling at its mother's breast. Naturally, the parents were extremely anxious. This is when Lal Ded appeared on the scene, took the infant in her arms, and said, 'You have not felt shy of being born; then why do you feel shy of tasting the pleasures of this world?' She then placed the child's mouth to her own breast, and gave him his first drop of food. As she left, Lal Ded told Sadra: 'Take great care of my spiritual heir.' Salar and Sadra named their child 'Nund', or the pious one. The name Nuruddin, or the light of the faith, was given to the child by Syed Hussain Simnani. [10]

In Nuruddin Rishi, ordinary Kashmiris find hope. He is responsible for having created the order of the Rishis[11] in the valley, and, in fact, took the work of his mentor a step further. He strived to create a union between the existing religions and the new-found Bhakti movement. Following in the footsteps of Lal Ded, the saint was Shaikh to his Muslim followers and Nand Rishi to the Hindus.

Having followed the same mystics – both man and woman – something must have horribly shaken the foundations of Hindus and Muslims in Kashmir to have come to a point where the former had no choice but to leave the land. Was a political ideology that underlined extremist undertones dominant around the time the Pandits were asked to leave the valley? How did that ideology germinate, and who were the instigators behind the forced exodus? The following pages will seek to find answers to these questions. But before that, let's explore, very briefly, the modern history of Kashmir, beginning 1946.

The state of Jammu and Kashmir consists of three main lands: the valley of Kashmir, Jammu and Ladakh. Due to extreme weather conditions, Jammu is the winter capital, while Srinagar remains the summer capital. The shift from one city to the other is referred to as the moving of the *durbar* or the assembly, lending an aristocratic air to the entire process. While each mainland has its own issues, the valley remains most affected by the Kashmir conflict. Jammu and its adjoining areas grudge the fact that India, and the rest of the world, do not acknowledge the impact of the conflict on them. Ladakh has always resented the step-child treatment meted out to it, and its internal clashes of philosophy between Buddhist-dominated Leh and Muslim-dominated Kargil have ensured very little progress in terms of development. While the main cities of Srinagar, Jammu and Leh remain tourist hotspots, and have therefore been greatly influenced by the outside world, the rest of J&K almost remains virgin land in terms of tourism, and therefore these areas harbour pristine natural beauty.

In 1946, when the British decided to partition India, they could only influence 54 per cent of the Indian subcontinent to bow to their wishes, as the remaining 46 per cent was administered by the British through treaties, and included large 'Princely States' – J&K was one of the 564 such states. Under the Cabinet Mission Plan of May 1946, British paramountcy over these states would lapse with Britain's departure, making them independent, although they were given the option to join the Indian or Pakistani state through a new federal relationship or other political arrangements.[12]

While India and Pakistan were still negotiating, Kashmir – which was then ruled by Maharaja Hari Singh – was disinterested in either. The Maharaja hoped for independence, and had signed a Standstill Agreement with both countries. 'But it was obvious that at some point, rather sooner than later, the future of Jammu and Kashmir would be placed on a table at which both India and Pakistan would be seated. But time did not stand still for Pakistan. It sought to win by war what it might conceivably have obtained through peace. That war has not ended.'[13]

Those at loggerheads over Kashmir in pre-Partition India were political entities: the Indian National Congress and the Muslim League. The Congress, under the leadership of Jawaharlal Nehru, aimed to unify the princely states, bring them under the banner of the Indian Union, and consolidate India's frontiers. The Muslim League, headed by Muhammad Ali Jinnah, firstly aimed at realizing its political dream: the creation of Pakistan. After this was realized, the second aim of the Muslim League was to 'prevent the consolidation of India and to balkanize it, if possible'[14] in order to make the differences in size and population between India and Pakistan seem unimportant.[15]

As Indian and Pakistani nationalists battled to consolidate their respective frontiers in the run-up to the Partition, Kashmir began to take on even greater importance. J&K was not only the largest princely state in India, but it bordered USSR, China and Afghanistan, and was part of the caravan trade route from Central Asia to India. For both India and Pakistan, it was essential to control the state to secure their borders.[16] Kashmir was also important for its water resources. The state was consequently considered a new source of vulnerability for Pakistan, and its accession to that country an 'absolute necessity for (its) separate existence'.[17]

Pakistan sent Afghani and/or Pathani tribal raiders, *kabailis*, in the third week of October 1947, who attacked Kashmir simultaneously on various frontiers, hoping to annex the state. The strategy failed in its larger objective. The Maharaja did not buckle under pressure and accede to Pakistan. Instead, he signed the Treaty of Accession[18] with India, after which Indian troops came to his aid and defeated the raiders in the first war over the Himalayan territory, though Pakistan managed to seize and retain control over PAK and the Northern Areas. However, the legality and authenticity of the Treaty of Accession has long been a subject of much debate.[19] Perhaps the bigger tragedy in Kashmir, other than the conflict and the subsequent loss of life and faith, has been that every action, no matter how well-intended, has been subject to disputes and contestations.

The choice of the Maharaja to sign the treaty, never formally acknowledged by Pakistan, has led to four wars between India and Pakistan. The first war ended in 1949, when the United Nations (UN) arranged a ceasefire and set up a truce boundary line that gave India control of two-thirds of the disputed territory, and Pakistan the rest. The Kashmir issue remains one of the longest pending issues on the UN's table, almost as old as the organization itself. The UN mediators had also called for a referendum by Kashmir's citizens to decide their future, but it was never held, because the conditions for the referendum – including the complete withdrawal of Pakistani troops, as well as tribal and other Pakistani nationals 'not normally resident' in J&K, from the territory, and a reduction of Indian troops to the force 'considered necessary to assist local authorities in the observance of law and order'[20] – were never met.

India claims Kashmir is its integral part and vital for its secular fabric, even though the word 'secular' was added to the Preamble to the Constitution only as late as 1976, through the forty-second Amendment Act.[21] Pakistan, on the other hand, claims that since the majority of the population in Kashmir is Muslim, the state rightly belongs to it, according to the Two-Nation theory.[22] Kashmiris, however, do not accept these claims or the *status quo*.

This leads us to a crucial question: Is the so-called 'Kashmir problem' a mere issue of Hindu–Muslim disharmony?

> 'What happens to the state of Jammu and Kashmir? Should it be given to India or to Pakistan, become independent or be repartitioned? This Kashmir problem has kept lawyers, diplomats and writers busy since 1947. Over the last 54 years this problem has become rather abstract, debated by one country – Pakistan – that has usually spoken about the past without reference to the present and by another – India – that talks about Kashmir only in the present (post-1971) without reference to the past. To outsiders the issue is reduced simply to geography and geopolitics.
>
> The second problem is far more complicated, interesting and pressing – the problem of Kashmiris themselves. How do Kashmiris get the government they want? The origins of the militancy that has since 1988 claimed more than 35,000 lives lie here. Yet this can be the only source of an enduring solution.'[23]

Article 370 of the Indian Constitution grants special status to J&K. According to it, the Indian Parliament needs the State Government's approval for applying all other laws other than in matters of defence, foreign affairs and communications. Thus, Kashmiris live under a separate set of laws, including those related to citizenship, ownership of property and fundamental rights, as compared to other Indians.[24]

Since 1989, the low-intensity conflict in J&K has been the most important issue in India's internal security scenario.[25] Pakistan set out to channelize civilian discontent in the Indian-administered territory into an armed insurgency against India. Having successfully aided and abetted the jihad against Soviet presence in Afghanistan by arming and training the Afghan mujahideen, Pakistan set up several training camps on the same model on its territory for disaffected elements who were willing to take up arms against India's control in J&K.

The constant supply of terrorists generated from religious institutions in Pakistan and Afghanistan helped keep up the violence, despite the fact that Indian security forces succeeded in neutralizing a substantial number of terrorists every year. Undoubtedly, the civilian population has been most affected by the insurgency in J&K. While human casualty is one consequence, refugee generation and economic stagnation are the others. Tourism, the main economic activity in the state, has been affected adversely by terrorism.

I had written down in my little notebook my initial observations of the very first visit to J&K in 2003:

> 'Across the bustling city, at every kilometre or so, a soldier or a paramilitary gunman stands strapped in a 28-kg bulletproof jacket, holding an assault rifle, his finger caressing the trigger, furtively looking in every direction. Others stand trapped in bunkers, a web of barbed wires across a small opening, the barrel of a gun jutting

through it. The mesh of wires is to bounce off a grenade that could be lobbed at them anytime. Some others stand inside drums in the middle of the road. Only their heads in helmets are visible, watching out for a speeding car bomb. There are bunkers and camps inside the maze of bylanes in residential colonies, holding their space, like little "green zones" in the Baghdad of India. Not that I am a blind nationalist, but more than 25 years and India has not been able to win over the people of Kashmir one bit? We are where we were when the first shots were fired in November 1989. What an abysmal failure of the mandarins of our foreign policy and internal security. It takes a blink of an eye for 5,000 people to storm the streets of any Kashmiri city. And you call this normalcy?'

In what can be termed as the turmoil's most violent face, the casualties – along with human lives – have been trust, confidence, brotherhood and the ethos of Kashmiriyat. It is not an exaggeration to say that Indian security personnel have been insensitive, brutal and ruthless in dealing with the issue. Reports of fake encounters, mistaken identities and the most gruesome forms of torture in the name of security issues are abundant. It may be interesting to note that though atrocities have been committed both by the security forces as well as by the militants, only the ones committed by the former get highlighted.

The response of the security forces has resulted in a complete loss of faith in the Indian legal system, further alienation of Kashmiris, immense hatred for the Indian state and, most importantly, unbelievable human rights violations. Every single household in Kashmir has been affected by the conflict, and life for an average Kashmiri seems to be an endless period of waiting. For the half-widows of Kashmir, it is a traumatic and uncertain wait for news of their 'disappeared' husbands; 'political prisoners' await return to their homes; parents wait for their 'disappeared' sons to return; the numerous women who have been sexually harassed wait for the perpetrators of the crimes to receive punishment; surrendered militants await a day when they would not have to report to the local police station and be subjected to the choicest treatment every time there is a violent incident in their neighbourhood; 'misguided' youth await a time when they can return to their motherland; Kashmiri Pandits wait to return to the valley.

There have been several stakeholders in the making of the present-day J&K, Sheikh Mohammad Abdullah being one of them. It is not within the scope of this book to delve into the political nature of and the role played by this extraordinary Kashmiri. Yet, he is someone who has single-handedly influenced the turn of events in the land's history, whether it be the renaming of the Muslim Conference as the National Conference in 1938; introducing the controversial Land Reform Movement in 1931,[26] which ensured the transfer of land from the feudal lord to the peasant; or an open rejection of the Two-Nation theory at a historic rally in Srinagar in October 1947, soon after his release from Maharaja Hari Singh's jail.

Ordinary Kashmiris were thoroughly confused by Sheikh Abdullah's acts. Without being given an option, they found themselves shouldering the responsibility of having to maintain and balance the see-saw between India and Pakistan, the contested object being Kashmir itself. Their notion about India was thus: a land of many cultures, languages and identities. To them, it was clear why India wanted Kashmir. Adding Kashmir to its kitty would strengthen India's secular and sovereign image in front of the entire world. Their notion about Pakistan was: a land which understood its culture, based on Islam. For them, Pakistan wanted Kashmir because it wanted the people of Kashmir to be able to freely practice their religion and live in peace.

Based on these notions, ordinary Kashmiris supported and strengthened Pakistan's efforts to infiltrate into the Indian-administered regions of Kashmir, with men and women alike supporting the turmoil. While the men crossed over to Pakistan-administered Kashmir (also known as 'Azaad' Kashmir) to receive training in arms, and came back to 'liberate' their motherland from India, the women were at the forefront of protests and rallies and provided much-required psycho-social support to the men. In turn, the men got killed and the women bore the brunt of it in the form of the most gruesome human rights violations.

In any society, women – consciously or unconsciously – strengthen existing social structures. In J&K, they do much more. Contrary to popular perception, women's issues are not a 'soft' subject matter, but a plethora of complex themes with unimaginable parameters, and this is especially true of women in J&K.

In March 2004, a bill called the J&K Women's Permanent Resident (Disqualification) Bill was moved in the J&K legislature. According to the bill: 'Notwithstanding anything contrary contained in any law... a female permanent resident on her marriage with a person who is not a permanent resident shall with effect from the date of such marriage cease to be permanent resident.' This bill was passed in the Lower House. A major controversy followed, due to which it was not passed in the Upper House, and therefore did not become a law.

Proposed and endorsed by the Jammu and Kashmir People's Democratic Party as well as the National Conference, the bill was opposed by both the Congress and the BJP. Of course, women's groups opposed it vehemently.

Another failed attempt was made to pass the bill again, in 2010. As of now, women in J&K retain their permanent resident status, even after they marry a non-state subject. But the fact is that women's position in Kashmiri society remains an issue of discussion, and a debatable one too.[27]

I am reminded of a time when I was a part of a team that organized an inter-faith workshop for a diverse group of men and women from different religious backgrounds from J&K, in Delhi in 2004. I was recently reminded of this group by the Bollywood film *Kurbaan*, which portrays Muslims stereotypically. More specifically, it places Muslim women in the typical fashion where they simply toe the line of their men. I wondered aloud with a friend if we would be embarrassed to watch the film with any of our Kashmiri friends, particularly the women!

Kashmiri women were politically the most active in the early '90s. The image of Kashmiri women – over the past two decades – has been that of mothers, wives and daughters covered from head to toe, leading protest marches and facing the blows of police batons. Such images regularly filled the pages of local and national newspapers. Srinagar used to be flooded with women everyday in early '90s and the streets reverberated with the slogan: '*Marde mujahid jag zara ab, waqt-e-shahadat aaya hai*! (Awaken you holy fighters as the time has come for martyrdom!)' Such activism was perhaps a liberating experience for most women.

This immediately brings to my mind an interaction with Sharadaben, a Vishwa Hindu Parishad (VHP) activist, whom I met in Ahmedabad, Gujarat. Her association with the Rashtriya Swayamsevak Sangh's (RSS) right-wing Hindu-extremist outfit was a matter of great pride for her. 'I've been with the VHP for 35 years now,' Sharadaben told me in her house in the suburbs of Ahmedabad. 'We don't get any money from the VHP for doing *kar-seva*. We simply do it because of our love for our Hindu brothers and sisters. We believe in doing service from the heart... We can enforce peace, and we can also create violence. We are not scared of going to riot areas and taking charge.' I asked her to explain her statement. 'The head office gives us orders, and we follow. Whether they ask us to go for a protest march or to participate in violence against Muslims, we don't question the head office. We simply follow orders. We were there when the demonstrations were going on during the Ram Setu (Sethusamudram) controversy; we were there when the Babri Masjid was being demolished.' The pride in her voice was unmistakable. 'I am not afraid of dying. You only live once and die once. So either die or kill. When I'm doing *kar-seva,* I don't care even if my saree comes undone.' Sharadaben was obviously ideologically driven to believe in and do what she did.

Coming back to Kashmir and its women, they have supported the 'freedom movement' in broadly four ways: they have acted as motivators to provide support to those fighting the war for liberation from India. Convinced of the role of jihad and jihadis, women have provided psychological support to Kashmir's men as mothers, sisters and wives. The mujahideen have been glamourized and projected as heroes. To be identified as mother/sister/aunt of a jihadi has been a matter of great pride for Kashmiri women. Traditional Kashmiri folklore or *wanwun* of the early 1990s is a typical and accurate example of this:

*Yim mujahid zoraware, Yem kapaise aayaie*
*Yim aayi sarhad pareyaie, Tim kapare aaie*
*Sopore kerekh cross-firing, Waremuli kerekh chaire*
(These powerful mujahids, where did they come from?
They came from across the border, from the other side.
They resorted to cross-firing at Sopore, and took tea at
Baramulla.)

*Kalashnikov lagai balayai*
*Yenav ladayat path fairaleh*
(Don't give up this fight for freedom;
I shower my life on this Kalashnikov!)

*Main mujahidov behan*
*Praraie hideoutas*
(O my beloved mujahid,
I will wait for you at the hideout.)

*Wanwun* compositions were earlier sung at weddings and other celebrations. As one of the biggest tributes to Lal Ded, they are never written, but are composed on the spur of the moment. The tune of all the songs is more or less the same. Between stanzas, there is a gap of a few seconds during which the women, who alone sing these songs standing and holding each other by the waist, compose the next line.

Life mirrors reality. As they say, so it happens. Over the past many years of an anti-India revolt in Kashmir, lyrics of traditional songs of celebration have given way to ghastly changes:

*Saien tehreekh kya chhaie*
*Jaan waisiwaye*
*Asi me marew ase chhe*
*Insaan wasiswaye*
(Our struggle for freedom is genuine.
So why do you torture us for that?
We are humans, too!)

Instances of women providing shelter and food to militants and protecting them from security forces are common. Whether they did this out of choice or due to lack of one is highly debatable. Young Kashmiri girls romanticized the idea of falling in love with a mujahid, and many eventually did run away and/or marry them, lured by the risk and glory that came with such an association. However, in one particular incident in early 2006, in village Darhal, district Rajouri, a young girl was able to convince her mujahid suitor to give up arms if he wanted to marry her!

In the case of young men who became 'martyrs' for the Kashmiri cause, their mothers were almost worshipped. Huge crowds gathered when militants' bodies were brought to their houses. The mothers were often heard making statements which glorified the dead men and how lucky they were to have birthed a martyr. In an article written by Arif Shafi Wani of *Greater Kashmir* on 27 November 2006, and posted on the Kashmiri Global Network called Kashnet, 'Sara, 65, mother of a slain JKLF (Jammu and Kashmir Liberation Front) militant, Mushtaq Ahmad Kutay, said: "I am proud that my son laid his life for freedom of Kashmir."' Mushtaq was among the seven militants, including JKLF commander Sheikh Abdul Hamid, killed during a boat capsizing after an encounter at Aali Kadal on 19 November 1992. '"Ten days were left for Mushtaq's marriage when he left home on some mission. Before leaving, I offered him sweets and kissed him," Sara recounts. "I did not weep when his body was brought home. Instead, I offered prayers at Dastgeer Sahib to thank Allah as my son laid his life for a noble cause," she said.'[28]

Another way in which women supported the freedom struggle was by raising their voices against human rights violations in Kashmir. According to a senior police officer, women often registered FIRs (First Information Reports) stating that a person had gone missing, even when the person was actually operating as a militant. Women also pursued cases for the release of their sons and/or husbands. This 'activism' was running parallel to the struggle for freedom. It was also not uncommon for Kashmiri women to allege rape by security forces. And in some cases, the allegations were not true. In fact, they were encouraged to give testimonies against violations committed by Indian security forces, and were used as victims and targets of the Indian agenda.

The formation of women's activist groups like the Dukhtaran-e-Millat (DeM) and Muslim Khwateen Markaz (MKM) was a big event in the political history of Kashmir, and the third way in which women supported the insurgency movement. In September 1995, the DeM was held responsible for a bomb blast that killed Mushtaq Ali, a photographer from Agence France Presse (AFP), in Srinagar. According to news reports, a woman dressed in a burqa entered the BBC/Reuters office in Srinagar and introduced herself as a member of DeM. She dropped off a parcel addressed to Yusuf Jameel, the BBC and Reuters correspondent in Kashmir. Instead, Ali opened the package, which promptly exploded, killing him and injuring two others. The DeM denied responsibility for the attack, but it is highly likely that the perpetrator of the bombing was a member of the group.

The MKM president, Mohtarma Bakhtawar, popularly called Behenji, got immense mileage and became a household figure after she saved the life of JKLF chief Hamid Sheikh. It was not uncommon to sight *chadar*-shrouded MKM activists acting as guards to militants, intimating them of the approach of security forces and giving them ample time to escape. MKM activists were routinely spotted providing physical support in the form of food and clothes to jailed militants and would even collect money for bail.

Ordinary women found themselves carried away by the emotional high of activism almost overnight and became activists. The there are numerous instances where women have been used as carriers of money, and other individual instances of support extended by women. Dardpora, commonly known as the 'village of half-widows', in Kupwara, is very close to the Line of Control (LoC), the de facto border. Almost all its men have been killed either in fratricidal wars or by Indian security forces in the early years of militancy. Widowhood has become the dominant marker of the women from Dardpora. According to unconfirmed reports, the half-widows here made some easy money by showing shortcuts in the mountains to militants.

In the Avantipura explosion, which happened soon after the October 2005 earthquake in Kashmir, a woman blew herself up on National Highway 1-A that connects the Kashmir valley to India. The Pakistan-based Jaish-e-Mohammed (JeM) claimed it was a *fidayeen* (suicide squad) attack, and the woman, Yasmeena Akhtar, was a suicide bomber. But investigations have yet to establish whether Yasmeena was actually a suicide bomber or whether she was merely transporting explosives from one place to another, and whether the explosion occurred due to a mistake on her part. Media reports, however, clearly pointed towards Yasmeena's involvement much beyond that of a mere transporter. The JeM actually hailed her as the first woman suicide bomber, with many more to come!

However, there is little evidence to substantiate that women have actually picked up guns and resorted to violence in the name of Kashmiri nationalism. Several factors contributed to women getting swayed into supporting the insurgency. The politics of everyday life and survival was, perhaps, the most crucial one. Education, or the lack of it, helped various agencies to influence women and mould their thinking and subsequent behaviour in their favour. The absence of organized women's groups working for gender justice and equality and the subsequent emergence of fundamentalist women's groups like DeM and MKM played on the women's psyche as well. But above all, human rights violations were perhaps the single-most important factor in driving women to rebellion.

When Kashmiri women realized there were multiple militant groups present on the scene and foreign militants were not really fighting for the cause of Kashmir and were in fact only mercenaries, they stopped supporting them. It suddenly seemed as if it was in the interest of everyone to keep the Kashmir conflict alive. For the politicians, it was a big enough cause to harp on in international conferences; for the media, it was a big event to report on; for the militants, it was big money. The biggest tell-tale sign was when the fire of the struggle began to engulf the very Kashmiris who had been promised liberation. Initially, Pakistan had encouraged and trained Kashmiri youth from within the Indian state of J&K to fight against India and Indian security forces. Gradually, the misguided youth was then briefed to extend the periphery of their attacks, to the effect of hurting Kashmiris: men, women and children.

Meanwhile, Kashmiri 'freedom fighters' had developed their own ideologies and continued to fight their battle in their own way. This simultaneous clash at several levels between different agencies fighting for the 'Kashmir cause' destroyed the social fabric of Kashmir. The Azaadi dream evaporated quickly. The Pakistan dream also evaporated, as Kashmir realized Pakistan was not fighting for and on behalf of the people of Kashmir.

Its motive was the accession of the land, and it was willing and prepared to get it, no matter what the cost.

The year is 2008. I sit with a friend and his family in their home in Pandrethan, close to the Badami Bagh cantonment. From the window on the first floor of Khurram's house, one can see the faint line of the mountains, haloed by blobs of clouds. As the day turns from evening to dusk, the stillness of the city skyline is ruptured by the call for the prayers, *maghrib ki namaaz*. Soon, multiple azaans echo through the concrete jungle. In the 1990s, these minarets spread the message of Azaadi, when hordes of gun-toting youth gushed out of the bylanes to the city square and randomly fired in the air, chanting, 'Azaadi, Azaadi'. The day would shake with the rat-a-tat-tat of gunshots interspersed by an occasional thunder of a bomb, a never-ending Diwali. 'Now it is all quiet. Much, much less,' says Khurram's mother. Just a few years ago, there were three to four incidents every day in Srinagar. They've come down to one or two a *month*! But the feeling of alienation remains. If you ask Kashmiris if they want to be with India, they say 'no'. They don't want to be with Pakistan either; they want freedom.

It is 2013 now. I have come back to Kashmir after two long years. I feel like a prodigal daughter... Waking up to the sounds of the azaan in Kashmir is something which I have accepted unquestioningly, without giving it any thought. But as I open my eyes to the sounds this morning, something is not quite the same. As the sun climbs up from behind the Zabarwan hills visible from the window of Mushtaq's house, one of my many homes in Kashmir, I realize it isn't the muezzin calling the faithful to come and pray. It takes me several seconds to realize that the chorus of voices is from the aarti, prayers that Hindus sing in praise of their gods and goddesses. It feels surreal, to say the least! Hindu prayers in a Muslim land...

I have no specific plans for the day. I find myself sitting on Peerzu island, on the banks of the Jehlum, with a book on Rumi and his guru, Shams of Tabriz – *The Forty Rules of Love*. As I read about Rumi, Tabriz, Sufism, Christianity, Islam and much more, the sounds of azaan finally come floating on the waters of Jehlum, taking my thoughts to this morning's aarti. If this is not Kashmiriyat, I wonder what is!

Let us take a look at the status of women in traditional Kashmiri society, much before the seeds of the current turmoil were sown, using the case studies of two women who not only find mention in the history of Kashmir – for political as well as other reasons – but are also exemplary in the way they chose to lead their lives.

The sixteenth century Kashmiri poet and literary figure Habba Khatun was born in a small village called Chandrahar. A peasant girl then called Zoon, she learnt how to read and write. An early marriage, and an unhappy one, led to her disillusionment with life. Zoon returned to her parents' house, and spent her days composing poetry. Yusuf Shah Chak, who was to later become Kashmir's ruler, saw Zoon singing her poems about lost love, and fell in love with her. He convinced her to marry him, and soon the peasant girl became the Maharani of Kashmir, Habba Khatun. She was renowned as much for her beauty as for her verses, and is said to have introduced to the Kashmiri language the *lol*, which is almost like the 'lyric' in English.

Soon, the Mughals took over Kashmir. Akbar seized power, and after arresting Yusuf Shah Chak, sent him to languish in a jail in Bihar. Habba Khatun went to Delhi and Bihar looking for her husband, but to no avail. Yusuf Shah died in jail, and Habba Khatun died lamenting for her husband, singing songs that spoke of the sorrow of separation. The pathos and emotions she brought forth in her poetry is clearly indicative of her loss and suffering. While her earlier works speak of lost love and the sufferings of a broken heart, her later poems have a much stronger base where she makes it clear that she is not willing to compromise on any front. Perhaps this was a message to the Mughals, who believed in seizing everything by the force of war. For Habba Khatun to express her feelings in times of political turmoil and unrest through her poems and songs is remarkable.

Yet another popular figure in Kashmir is singer Malika Pukhraj. Born in Hamirpur Sidhdhar village, close to Akhnoor, in the early twentieth century, Malika started singing at the court of Maharaja Hari Singh very early in life. She received an education in Urdu and Persian, and also learnt the nuances of music and dance from several renowned gurus of her time. Since Pukhraj was part of the court, she also developed an interest and a distinct and characteristic lifestyle pertaining to politics and current affairs. The Maharaja took her along with him wherever he went, and in a candid account of her life in her memoir *Song Sung True*,[29] Pukhraj gives a detailed description of not just her own life, but also how the kingdom of J&K was run during those times.

Coming back to the present scenario, and observing this in the light of some of the women who have had a strong impact on J&K, one dimension that has been missing from the national and international radars is the impact of the conflict and violence on Kashmiri women and the fact that they have had to take on so many roles in the absence of their men, leaving them with almost no space to mourn the losses they've suffered. Travelling in rural Kashmir, I had one primary observation – the women of Kashmir are the most affected and silent sufferers of an extended turmoil. As they don't form a strong vote bank, no political party fights for their rights and no social group is willing to take up their cause.

As a keen observer and follower of the women's movement, my work with the women in Kashmir naturally and instinctively developed a feminist undertone. The women's movement in India can broadly be divided into three segments – first, urban feminist groups; second, the larger, more rural-oriented voluntary organizations; and third, the mass peasant struggles. In a place like J&K – a territory torn by conflict – mobilization of women's rights is next to impossible. Issues of violation of women's rights do get raised within the context of identity politics, but the concern for women does not go beyond a cursory point. Yet, across the state, women have built platforms for peace, rebuilt communities blown apart by separatist agendas (especially in the case of Kashmiri Pandits) and nurtured those who have been scarred in unimaginable and innumerable ways, slowly building a structure of 'normalcy' under the most difficult conditions.

The idea of documenting the kinds of issues Kashmiri women face in their day-to-day lives crept into my thoughts while organizing a travelling exhibition of posters from the women's movement in India, aptly titled 'Poster Women', in the valley towards the end of 2007. Initiated by the Delhi-based feminist press, Zubaan, the Poster Women project began with the idea of locating and archiving posters from across India from the early '70s, a period that is characterized as having given rise to the women's movement in India.

This exhibition travelled to many cities within the country with the aim of highlighting the Indian woman's fight against a patriarchal society. The idea was for people – both men and women – to be aware of the different issues faced by women in general. The exhibition aimed at inspiring them by introducing the history of Indian women's struggle for equal rights, family planning, reproductive rights, the banning of invasive contraceptives, access to health facilities, literacy, environment, political participation and also against domestic violence, communalism and marginalization.

When the posters were exhibited in the valley, I tried to locate Kashmiri women's groups who might want to contribute to the existing collection; I found none. While there are numerous issues that women in J&K face – issues that have arisen out of the conflict, and issues that women face because they are women – there is no documentation or even acknowledgement of these.

However, work on conflict in the past two decades has looked at the specific implications of conflict for women. Feminist writing has attempted to understand the politics of mothers' fronts; the specific mobilizations by women to promote peace and resist conflict; the ways in which family and community locks women into inescapable custody through non-consensual marriage; the denial of choice in widowhood and remarriage practices; the experiences of combatant women within militant movements and resistance struggles; and the relationship between the violent masculinity of the armed forces and women at contested boundaries or on the borders of nations, to list but a few concerns in the subcontinent.

Most of the developmental work in and around conflicts approaches the issue from an invariable and crude notion of identity. We need to perhaps view it from the notions of masculinity and femininity – separating women's issues from the rest of it – and their connections with violence or peace. But what needs to be done right away is to interact with common men and women in Kashmir and make them feel 'involved'.

This book attempts, more than anything else, to look at the Kashmir 'conflict' from the point of view of those who have been neglected – the women. What has Azaadi meant to them? How have they transcended the various boundaries between them and their Azaadi? Has this elusive Azaadi been worth all the brutality, bloodshed and battle? For obvious reasons, the book is valley-centric, but I have included in it my experiences of working and interacting with women from Jammu and Ladakh as well.

However, this book is not a political account of the history of the land and its many rulers. It is also not a day-to-day commentary on the many incidents of turmoil and turbulence that J&K has witnessed – political, communal, personal or otherwise. It does not give an updated version of the latest developments in the Kashmir conflict, or the brutalities inflicted upon its people, the reason being that this book is meant to bring out women's voices in contrast to those of men, who have so far dictated the narrative of the Kashmir conflict.

My 'induction' into the valley happened thus: An elderly man, whose *shikara* I had hired, asked me: 'So, you are from India?' I wasn't sure what he meant, but his hostility fell into perspective very soon. Over the years, I have had the privilege of meeting and interacting with thousands of people from Jammu, Kashmir and Ladakh, and I have experienced hostility and hospitality, both at once and at very close quarters, and both for very different reasons in each of the regions. This, to me, is the most captivating aspect of being involved with a place and its people who have never been rid of 'trouble', at least not in the last few decades.

I was once reading a book where the author wrote a rather long, interesting narrative about what place does she call 'home'. Naturally, I found myself dwelling on the same question. I am a through-and-through Delhi 'product', having been born and brought up in the national capital, but my family comes from Sindh, Pakistan. Like millions of others, my grandparents, too, travelled the torturous and painful road called the Partition, and found themselves on this side of the border. My childhood was full of stories from Sindh. As I grew up in New Delhi, I could see myself nowhere else but in Delhi. My husband, however, belonged to Lucknow. So what does that make me? Which place is 'home' to me?

Kashmir is the land I dream of most nights. This is the land where I have mentally ticked places I want my daughter to visit. This is the land which has adopted me, given me a refuge whenever I've needed one. It is my *karmabhoomi*, my *junoon*; of course, Kashmir is my 'home'. It is a beautiful realization to know this. However, it took several years and many experiences for it to dawn on me.

During a bus journey from Srinagar to Doda, a fellow passenger asked me, 'Are you a Kashmiri?' I replied, 'Yes, by profession'. It immediately reminded me of that first question: 'So, you are from India?' On another trip, this time from Rajouri to Poonch, again on a local bus, I was spoken to in Kashmiri. I smiled back politely. Though I don't speak the language, I do understand some of it. These two incidents, to me, represented my being 'accepted' into the land by its people. Of course, on my part, I have made sincere and genuine attempts to be one amongst them – by dressing the way they do, covering my head when the occasion demands, trying to imitate the so-very-Kashmiri accent...

In the autumn of 2008, I was visiting J&K after a gap of a year. I was recovering from a personal tragedy, and before I went to Kashmir, I wasn't sure I could, or should, do so. But I realized I had nothing to lose, and no one to stop me, so I did make that trip. And today, I am glad I did. Because it was there that I found my bearings again. There was newfound meaning and purpose. Without being aware of it at that point in time, Kashmir was healing my injured soul and making it whole again.

A few months later, on my next visit to Srinagar, I was wandering around aimlessly in Makhdoom Sahib's dargah in Srinagar, and thereafter in the ruins next to it. It was then that it became clear to me: the fact that this relationship with Kashmir was not bound by time, distance, travel; it was here to stay despite all odds, and it was a relief to know that Kashmir was 'home'.

In school, during geography classes, one learnt about the physical boundaries of India. Its map began with J&K as its northern-most state. I accepted it the way it was, without any inkling of what lay within the so-called borders of J&K. My mind grasped the volatility of the word 'Kashmir' as I grew up and read disturbing reports about the violence and waste of human lives there.

Twenty-five odd years ago, when people's living rooms were not flooded with dozens of 24/7 news channels broadcasting 'breaking news', when Doordarshan was the only source of televised news, I remember sitting with my grandfather and watching the coverage of a communal massacre in J&K. My young mind did not fully fathom what was being telecast; yet the painful images and the shrieking cries of women made it clear to me that something very dreadful had happened.

As I grew up and made my way through school and college, Kashmir somehow took a backseat. I started working as a journalist, and it was then that Kashmir resurfaced in my life. When I was working as a sub-editor with the *Hindustan Times*, I recollect my desk editor screaming his lungs off at a colleague who, in the previous day's edition, had made an error while copy-editing a report on J&K. The desk editor shrieked: 'You have already given away Jammu and Kashmir to Pakistan!'

Moving from journalism to feminist publishing, Kashmir 'happened' quite suddenly and unexpectedly. Working on and around the women's movement, I was associated with several women's groups in New Delhi. I got the opportunity to work with WISCOMP (Women in Security, Conflict Management and Peace). This was the beginning of a challenging, mesmerizing and immensely emotional relationship with J&K. The days leading up to my first visit to the city of Srinagar, in May 2003, were spent dreaming and thinking only of what Kashmir would be like.

The first glimpse of Kashmir from the aircraft's window was an intense experience. Snow-capped Himalayan ranges became visible almost without a warning. The sight of them overwhelmed, intimidated and startled me, all at the same time. In contrast to the brown, patchy and rock-hard aerial view of New Delhi, Kashmir presented itself as a colourful mosaic with unmistakable patches of green. There were so many shades of green that I started counting them, but soon gave up because I could not keep pace!

As the aircraft prepared to land at Srinagar, the beautiful aerial landscape gave way to Army bunkers all along the runway. It was a different land from the one I had witnessed just two minutes ago. I collected my luggage and walked out of the airport. All this while, I had the uncomfortable feeling of being 'watched'. Hussain, my driver and guide, waited anxiously. The taxi negotiated its way through the roads of Srinagar, which appeared like any other commercialized city. Somehow, the presence of security personnel everywhere did not match my imagination of this summer capital. We were moving along the Dal Lake – lined with houseboats and shikaras – which was quite unlike the Dal of my imagination. I remember the disappointment of being in a Kashmir unlike what Jahangir's famous couplet said about the land: *Agar firdaus bar ru-e zamin ast, Hami ast o-hami ast o-hami ast* (If there is a paradise on earth, it is this... it is this... it is this...).

There are many hotels and guest houses in Srinagar to suit every budget. The one in which I settled during that maiden visit faced the Dal, and right behind it was the Shankaracharya hill, on top of which rested the Shankaracharya temple. Lord Shiva is said to have meditated here. From one of the windows in the hotel lobby, one could see the Hari Parbat fort – distant and majestic.

Hussain has, since that very first trip, remained my travel companion to many, many parts of the valley. His camaraderie, concern and guidance through the years have kept me going. Our conversations and discussions during long trips to faraway districts have been food for my soul. During one such trip to district Kupwara, a signpost read: 'Be gentle on my curves.' Hussain got so distracted by the signpost and my giggles that he missed a security personnel waving his lathi to stop us. When we realized what we had done and what the repercussions could be, my whole life ran in front of my eyes in a matter of a few seconds, almost like a movie clip. My thoughts were for my daughter whom I had promised a trip to the valley (a promise which was later fulfilled). Luckily, we escaped with some rude words thrown in our direction, an extra-thorough check of the vehicle, and threats to be more careful while driving around! As we moved on in our journey, the next signpost read: 'Driving is a pleasure when done at leisure!' I couldn't help but smile.

On my second trip to Kashmir, when I was still becoming aware of 'conflict zone vocabulary', I asked Mushtaq, a former senior journalist with the Reuters news agency: 'What does peace mean to you?' He was livid; he lost his cool and threw back the answer at me, which resounds in my head even now: 'The day we have no bomb blasts in Kashmir, and nobody is killed by the security forces – that will be peace to me.' Several years later, Mushtaq is family now, but the bitterness of that first meeting is unforgettable.

Another unforgettable memory from the same trip is my first shikara ride. A velvety lullaby: this is what crossed my mind as the sprawling, majestic Dal Lake cradled my boat, gently rocking it like a baby sleeping in its mother's lap. For miles, the bluish-grey water spread across like a sheen of tranquillity, cushioned by a sturdy line of high mountains on whose summits bundles of clouds hung motionless. The only sound was that of the slow, rhythmic flapping of the boatman's oars as they dipped into the water. I dozed off for a good half-an-hour, oblivious of the strains beneath this calmness, the shadow of violence lurking in the cool breeze blowing through the chinar trees, whose leaves were bursting to change colour from green to crimson. 'Peace', which appeared on the surface of Kashmir, too, seemed ready to burst into a riot of crimson, also the colour of blood. As if to signal how quickly the stillness in the valley could be shattered, a Central Reserve Police Force (CRPF) motorboat whirred at a distance – carrying men with AK-47s and binoculars, looking out for an unpredictable adversary who chose his own time and place to strike. At the same time, the famed flower market, on another boat, on the same Dal Lake, carrying beautiful, colourful flowers of different shapes and sizes, chose to cross paths with my shikara. As it floated away to an unknown, undisclosed and indescribable destination somewhere in the realms of the lake, the contrast between the CRPF boat and the flower boat on the same turf got registered subconsciously.

I have often faced the dilemma every researcher faces: How does one console somebody who has gone through a personal trauma like having lost someone in a bomb blast or in an encounter? What do you say when you want to sympathize, but you know that no matter what you say, you can never feel what the traumatized person or family is going through? And finally, when you are out in the field, gathering 'research material' for your own requirement, how do you not 'use' those affected merely for your own purpose? I don't think I will ever find answers to these questions. This book is a humble attempt to present a picture of Kashmir, especially its women, from the point of view of the women themselves, in the light of candour and compassion.

I've had several interesting experiences in Kashmir; experiences which one could only go through here and nowhere else. On the outskirts of Srinagar once, I saw many civilians poking the ground with a long stick. As usual, I turned to Hussain to seek answers as curiosity got the better of me. A little surprised at my ignorance, Hussain told me they were looking for mine fields, traps which may have been planted by militants during the night, using darkness as cover. He explained that the long sticks which were being used were attached to a tiny device which is supposed to detect 'danger'.

Something similar happened in Draba, where I had gone to find out more about an all-women's village defence committee. Once I reached Surankote in Poonch, I was stationed in Draba for two days before I could travel further up in the mountains to reach Kulali. I had to wait for the Sikh Regiment of 16 RR (Rashtriya Rifles) to carry out a ROP (road-opening patrol) to ensure that the road up to Kulali was not laced with land mines and/or explosives.

Once I started working in J&K, among the many intriguing stories about the land I heard was that Jesus Christ had lived in Kashmir, and had in fact died here. During the time that I heard this fable, 'Jesus's shrine' at Rozabal, in Khanyar, downtown Srinagar, was featured in *Lonely Planet*. Suddenly there was an increase in the influx of tourists to the valley, especially to Rozabal, resulting in authorities banning foreign tourists from visiting the medieval tomb. The story gained so much ground that the caretakers of the shrine had to lock the property, and nobody is allowed to enter it anymore. One can merely sneak a quick look through a window, and photography is out of the question.

My schooling years have been spent in convent schools, and Jesus has been an unquestioned, undisputed presence in my life. Naturally, this story about Jesus in Kashmir got the better of me and I decided to visit the shrine. I went to meet the caretaker,

Mohammed Amin Ringshawl, first, who firmly told me, 'It is the work of people associated with the tourist trade. They are misleading visitors and making them believe that Jesus was buried here.'

During a long discussion about the Rozabal shrine and similarities between Yus Asaf, the saint whose tomb the shrine is, and Jesus, Amin said, 'Jesus said: I would come back to earth before the world came to an end.' The shrine's premises were locked, and barbed wire prohibited anyone from entering the complex. Peeping through a window, I could see a wooden chamber placed over a tombstone, covered with a green cloth embroidered with verses from the Koran. I sent a silent prayer to Jesus, requesting him to take care of Kashmir and its people before mindless violence put an end to everything.

Talking to a few more people, both Kashmiris and non-Kashmiris, here's what I gathered: The idea that Jesus visited J&K and died here first arose in the mid-nineteenth century, when European scholars sought to explain similarities between Christianity and Buddhism. In 1968, Aziz Abdul Kashmiri published a book called *Christ in Kashmir*. 'Kashmiri history books tell us that Yus Asaf came from abroad. He came from Israel. He came to spread his teachings. He lived and died here. Yus Asaf was Issa. He was Jesus,' a report quoted Kashmiri as telling the BBC.

Those days, I happened to be reading a book called *Jesus Lived in India*, written by Holger Kersten. This was a follow-up on the visit to the 'tomb of Jesus'. The book mentions in great detail the travels of Russian historian Nicolai Notovitch, who travelled extensively throughout the state on one of his many journeys to the Orient. Whilst in Ladakh, Notovitch purportedly stumbled upon several leads which pointed towards Jesus having spent a lot of time in Kashmir and Ladakh. He believed Yus Asaf is Jesus, also because of the direction in which the grave is built, and the way in which the body is placed points towards a Jewish tradition, not Muslim. The following is an excerpt from his book, allegedly a dialogue between Notovitch and a lama at a Buddhist monastery:[30]

> 'You tell me that a son of Buddha, Issa, spread your religion over the Earth. Who is he, then?'

At this question the lama opened his eyes wide and looked at his visitor in astonishment. He explained:

> 'Issa is a great prophet, one of the first after the twenty-two Buddhas. He is greater than any one of the Dalai Lamas, for he constitutes part of the spiritual essence of our Lord. It is he who has enlightened you, who has brought back within the fold of religion the souls of the erring, and who allows every human being to distinguish between good and evil. His name and his deeds are recorded in our sacred writings.'

Notovitch was quite stunned at the lama's words, for the prophet Issa, his teaching, his martyrdom, and the reference to a Christian Dalai Lama were increasingly reminiscent of Jesus Christ.

It would be naive to assume that the transformation of the 'state of Jammu and Kashmir' into the 'Kashmir conflict' happened only once British India was divided into India and Pakistan. The troubled history of the region dates back to a time much before the Partition. However, the 'love-hate triangle' of India, Pakistan and Kashmir was born the minute there was talk of Partition.

What strikes me the most is the fact that even a twelve-year-old in Kashmir can give an account of the state's modern history. The reason, in the words of Prof. Abdul Ghani Bhat, a senior leader of the Hurriyat Conference, lies in the basic fact that not a single house in Kashmir has escaped the wrath of the conflict. We need to question ourselves as to whether we are even attempting to address the several conflicts going on in young, impressionable minds of Kashmir, since we are talking about those who will deal with the repercussions of the past and present in the near future.

It has been fascinating for me to undertake this journey into Kashmir through this book, visiting and revisiting incidents and occurrences in its history, the repercussions of which could be felt across the world. What is even more fascinating is to have done so with Kashmiri women, who have not just negotiated space for themselves amidst the trauma and turmoil of the conflict, but also held their places firmly. They have supported the Azaadi sentiment, fought for their place under the sun, protested and demonstrated in rallies while seeking justice for their men, and provided a motherly haven to their children. Over the years, the women have tried hard to douse the fires of violence, simultaneously keeping the fires in their houses burning. Each has emerged a winner in her own right, though somewhat bruised and shattered.

Most names of people and organizations in this book have been changed to protect their identities. However, each character is a real, living person, with whom I have had the privilege of sharing my Kashmir journey. This is a personal and intimate journey with each of the unique women. Through the narratives of these women, I have discussed, analysed and set out to explore what it means to be a woman in Kashmir, living in the midst of the conflict, amidst the half-truths and official lies, and amidst the chaos that governs everyday life. This book has also very briefly explored the role of women historically, and how that has changed and/or evolved after the conflict. Through the stories of these women, I have attempted to present a unique view of the conflict, reflected through the eyes of the marginalized, with the idea that the 'Kashmir issue' needs to be heard from the point of view of women, whose voices we don't hear at all, not even in the mainstream media.

Starting with a historical perspective on J&K in this introductory chapter, I have prepared the ground for introducing women in Kashmiri society. Using the case studies of Lal Ded, Habba Khatoon and Malika Pukhraj in this section, I have then attempted to set out a case for the sociological roles played out by the women, during the times of the current conflict, looking at a period from the early '90s onwards. This book is divided into sections titled 'Bhawani & Isbandh', 'Narcissus & Lotus', 'Humsaya & Boonye', 'Yogini' and 'Khanaqah & Ziyarat'. These are common words in the daily language of Kashmir. However, I have used them in very specific contexts – to describe the essential and basic character of each of the women protagonists in this book.

The beloved Mother Goddess is known by many names in Kashmir, one amongst them being Bhawani. Sudha Koul in her book *The Tiger Ladies* has beautifully described the Mother figure thus: 'She sits side-saddle or astride a demure tiger, her several arms hold everything vital to a good life. She Who Fears Nothing dismounts only to destroy evil wherever it hides its ugly self.'[31] Isbandh – also called *sangrani*, or incense – is burnt to create a joyous ambience as well as to ward off the evil eye and protect one's own. It is not difficult to imagine each and every Kashmiri woman donning the garb of the Mother and also burning her own self, if the need arises, to fiercely guard and protect her near and dear ones.

Few people are aware of an almost-established women's self defence corps in Kashmir as early as 1947, which was trained in the use of rifles in preparation for the war against Pakistani raiders. Though the women never fought at the battlefront, the whole exercise of learning how to use weaponry set the stage for their 'education' and therefore emancipation. The section 'Bhawani & Isbandh' looks at Kashmiri women and their role in the context of the late '80s and early '90s, a time marked by the re-emergence of disturbances. 'Azaadi' as a word had the capacity to start riots, define lifestyles, ignite (anti)nationalistic passions and transform, almost overnight, innocent, harmless people into future mujahids.

Taking this a step further, the same section looks at yet another organized effort on the part of women to use weaponry. The government of India advocated village defence committees

(VDCs) in the early '90s to combat militancy. VDCs comprise a group of villagers who are provided weapons and trained in their use by the government. These committees ceased to be male-dominated when the women of Kulali–Marrah took up guns in self defence.

The main player in the field during the early days of the insurgency was the Hizbul Mujahideen (HM), which consisted primarily of local Kashmiri men who were very clear that their war was against the Indian state and its so-called 'occupation' of their land. When the HM refused to inflict harm on local men and women, Pakistan introduced Afghani and/or Pakistani mercenaries, the Lashkar-e-Taiba (LeT), to the valley. Unfortunately, the stage was now set for the mass exodus of Kashmiri Hindus from the valley.

One of the reasons the movement slowed down was when a shift was brought about with foreign militants operating in the conflict. These militants did not have an emotional connect with either the land or its people. Not only did they demand food and shelter from the locals in the name of Islam, but also their daughters, sisters, wives and mothers. That is when the locals rose up and revolted against them to say that this was not the Islam they believed in. And this revolt was strongly backed by Kashmiri women.

The 'Bhawani & Isbandh' section views the world from the bitter perspective of a Kashmiri Pandit woman who lost her bearings as a child during the exodus. She comes back with a vengeance which is supported by education, exposure and scholarship. Sukanya Parashar, Zooni and Ananya Bhat alternate between the roles of Bhawani and Isbandh.

Narcissus, a white and yellow flower, originates from its namesake, a beautiful youth in Greek mythology who fell in love with his own image. The word is often associated with excessive interest in one's own self and appearance. I have contrasted this with the lotus, which is a large water lily. Again, in Greek mythology, the lotus's fruit induces a dreamy forgetfulness. The term 'lotus-eater' refers to a person who indulges in pleasure and luxury. Both flowers are to be found in abundance in Kashmir. While Narcissus, the Greek youth, obsessed with his own beauty, ends up drowning in the same water in which he sees his reflection and is mesmerized by it, every bit of the lotus plant is consumed in Kashmir. The flower is used for decoration; the stem is eaten as a vegetable, which is a local delicacy called *nadroo*; the leaves of the plant, twice the size of dinner plates, are used precisely for that, to eat off; the spongy, pod-like undergrowth of the plant is again a local delicacy, *pampach*, and is eaten as a fruit. While one is consumed by its own beauty (Narcissus), the other (Lotus) ends up being consumed by others. This contrast is especially true of Kashmiri women. Their beauty is unparalleled, and this same beauty gets marred by the daily clash of domesticity and the larger backdrop of the conflict.

The two protagonists in this section are Rafiqa and Zainab. Through the experiences of Rafiqa, I have attempted to understand a term which I have not yet fully comprehended – 'half-widow'. Her husband goes 'missing', and no one can say whether he is dead or alive. It is almost like the Hindu mythological character Trishanku, hanging between the earth and the sky; neither here nor there! According to the Association of Parents of Disappeared Persons (APDP), there are an estimated 2,000 to 2,500 such women who are unsure of their husbands' whereabouts and whether they are dead or alive.[32] The state's silence on this issue makes things worse. Through Zainab's life, I have focused on women as victims of the Kashmir conflict, especially when it comes to using sexual exploitation as a tool. The gruesome incident of the mass violation of women in Kunan Poshpora village is briefly revisited. Again, the state's stand on this particular incident is unpalatable! A part of this section also looks at selective memory as a tool to overcome trauma, in the cases of both Rafiqa and Zainab.

In Kashmir, there is a special word for neighbours and friends – *humsaaya*, or 'my very own'. Literally, it also means someone with whom one shares a roof. The lyrical connotation of this word is not simply music for the ears; it is a way of life in Kashmir. I have tried to, and haven't been able to, find a suitable equivalent of this word in the English language. At best, I could come up with 'a friend with who one shares a bond of mutual affection'; or 'someone who stands by you in your times of despair'; perhaps a selfless individual who does not judge you on the basis of your thoughts and actions. Actions speak louder than words in this case, especially when it comes to the women of Kashmir. To complement this nature of theirs is an equally mesmerizing word: *boonye*. The Chinar tree, which was originally brought to Kashmir from Persia by the Mughals, is an inseparable part of life in this land of exotic stories. Changing colours every season, its leaves turn a fiery red in the fall. In Kashmiri, the Chinar is called Boonye, and its abundant shade is the *shehjaar*, under which young boys play cricket with as much gay abandon as the women who get together for an informal session of *kahwa* and friendly neighbourhood gossip. An alternate term for Boonye could be comfort-provider.

This section captures the dilemma of Kashmiri women being mothers, wives, sisters and/or daughters waiting for the men to return from nowhere in particular, knowing very well that may never happen, yet never giving up hope. I have also described the land of Ladakh in 'Humsaya & Boonye', in the context of a natural calamity it faced in the year 2010. Recounting my experiences of having met different women in Leh and Kargil, the two main cities of Ladakh, I have tried to capture the land in its myriad moods. True to the name of the section under which their lives have been described, Jehanara Maqbool and Sonam Lobzang have sheltered and nurtured friends and family, even strangers, all their lives.

The word Yogini is self-explanatory: somebody who practices the art of Yoga, or self-discipline. A Yogini could also be someone who practices the highest levels of 'giving', of being 'selfless'. The section 'Yogini' in this book is a running commentary from the point of view of an old Kashmiri Pandit woman educationist – Sukanya Parashar – describing the Kashmir of yesteryears, and how the emergence of militancy quickly put an end to it.

In this section, I also introduce some young Kashmiri women who come as a breath of fresh air. These new-age women make their own decisions in life, have chosen atypical professions, following their hearts instead of the diktats of Kashmiri society, and are quite aware of the choices they have made in life. Roshan, Jahanavi, Firoza, Sophia and Aliya define a subtle change, at least the undercurrent of a change that is inevitable in the years to come, in Kashmir.

Kashmir is a land of spirituality, an amalgam of many cultures and religions. The land is dotted with several shrines, temples, mosques and other places of worship where people come searching for inner peace and salvation. Devotion towards not only one's own traditions but equal respect and reverence towards all other faiths is also practised here. Perhaps that is the reason why one finds so many *khanaqahs* and *ziyarats*, shrine complexes comprising mosques, tombs of saints, and reverence halls all built within the same complex. What better simile than these structures for the women of Kashmir, who are much more than mother-figures: they are providers, care-takers, shock-absorbers, as also victims and survivors, all at once. But to reach this level of being, each has had to go through her own journey, where there isn't always a companion with whom to share the travails of life. As a collective community, as the more marginalized and less noticed and understood sex, there has been a sense of similarity as far as each woman's path is concerned. Yet, each has had an individualistic encounter in terms of experiences with life and death.

This section of 'Khanaqah & Ziyarat' brings together all the protagonists from the different backgrounds under the common banner of what Azaadi means to each of these women, as also the notion of Kashmiriyat. A part of it sums up my personal association over a decade with the land and people of J&K, and my personal liberation, my very own Azaadi. It has been rather interesting for me to have studied the nature of conflict here, with a specific focus on the marginalized gender. Women's roles in the conflict, over the decades; their perspective and understanding of it; their reasons for why it emerged in the first place; how it has affected them and resulted in changes in their lives – some of these issues have also been explored in this section in the form of women's position in Kashmiri society post-2008. This partly autobiographical account of Kashmir will remain one of my most passionate works.

As I sit writing this in the walnut-wood-carved deck of my houseboat on Nagin lake, the sun has just slid behind a mountain, rendering a dash of orange and blue in the sky. It mirrored in the lake briefly, creating a halo of gold and blue on which my houseboat seemed anchored. The evening is once again punctured by the many sounds of the azaan from across Srinagar. The orange of the sun gives way to the silver of the moon. The evening is growing darker, and the moon is shining in its full glory. A childhood memory comes to me:

My father was driving us back home after a family outing. It was late evening, and the silvery light of the moon illuminated everything. To my young mind, it seemed strange that the moon was following us everywhere, no matter where we went and which turn we took! A deep sense of anxiety took over me, and I whispered the thought to my brother in the backseat of our military-green Fiat Padmini. When he was unable to explain why this was happening to us, I panicked. Realizing something was not quite all right, our mother turned around and asked us what the matter was. When I told my parents what was bothering me, they had a hearty laugh, and I was quite offended because they did not realize the gravity of the issue. Once we reached home, our father lovingly made us sit in his lap, and explained why the moon, the sun and the stars would continue to follow us everywhere, all our lives.

In Kashmir, where people are compelled to stay behind locked doors, particularly in the evenings, have Kashmiri children experienced the moon following them? The answer is a resounding 'no'. A sense of deep sadness prevails as I realize this. It is more likely that fathers have implored their children to remain quiet rather than encourage them to ask questions troubling their young minds.

In the context of Kashmiri women, I can't help but remember Agha Shahid Ali's lines in 'The Wolf's Postscript to Little Red Riding Hood':

> First, grant me my sense of history:
> I did it for posterity,
> for kindergarten teachers
> and a clear moral:
> Little girls shouldn't wander off
> in search of strange flowers,
> and they mustn't speak to strangers.

In the same breath, I sample these two telling comments from two different publications:

> The CRPF (Central Reserve Police Force), the BSF (Border Security Force) and the hordes of para-military outfits that have been raised by the government are better trained to rape women and kill unharmed villagers than to squarely face the dare-devil terrorists in Punjab and Kashmir.[33]

The Hizb-ul Mujahideen announced their goal of creating a *Nizam-e-Mustafa* (Islamic State) in the valley, and issued slogans like '*Agar Kashmir mein rehna hoga, Allah Allah kehna hoga*' (if you want to continue to live in Kashmir, you have to pray to none but Allah). [34]

While the first is an observation on the official state of affairs as far as security agencies are concerned, the second is a remark on the portrayal of a non-secular Kashmir, which was convenient for certain stakeholders in the conflict. The women of Kashmir have wrangled with both. This book is written in honour of the women, and in celebration of Kashmiriyat.

# Bhawani & Isbandh

*Up, woman! Go make your offering.*
*Take wine, meat and a cake fit for the gods.*
*If you know the password to the Supreme Place,*
*you can reach wisdom by breaking the rules.*[35]

Over the years, I've had the privilege of meeting and interacting with many Kashmiri women, and each one of them has helped me understand things from a 'woman's perspective'. After several informal chats and some heart-to-heart conversations, it made perfect sense why there were some women who supported the Azaadi sentiment but condemned the violence, some who supported the Azaadi sentiment as well as the violence and some who condemned both. What struck me most was that each one of them, without exception, had witnessed a violent incident, mostly involving close family members. It was chilling to observe that the women were bereft of any emotion while narrating the incidents. It was almost like they were so used to talking about the violence that it didn't stir them anymore!

Sukanya Parashar was one such woman. In her prime, she had been a part of what was called the Women's Self-Defence Corps, an all-women 'militia' group with both Muslim and Pandit women from all over Kashmir. It was raised with the active support of Sheikh Abdullah, the hero of the times and the man most Kashmiri women looked up to. The group was assembled to train women in self-defence and was raised in 1947 to combat the Pakistani *kabailis* or raiders who had invaded the valley after Partition in 1947.

When I met Sukanya at her Rajbagh residence in Srinagar, she was draped in a parrot-green cotton saree with a maroon Sambalpuri border. Eighty years old, she was elegance personified, and her every movement defined grace. She ensured we were comfortably seated in her sitting area which was tastefully decorated with plants, books and old artefacts. A strikingly beautiful younger woman served us tea and *nadroo* chips, a local delicacy made from the lotus stem, whilst Sukanya told me about the beginning of women's involvement in Kashmir's struggle for its own identity.

It took me a while to register that a women's brigade trained in the use of guns existed in Kashmir as early as 1947. What's more, they even knew how to blow up grenades! This mental image of the gun-toting Kashmiri woman was quite an antithesis to the *Kashmir ki kali* image I had in my mind. I was keen to know more, and Sukanya brought up names like Mahmooda

Ahmad Ali Shah, Krishna Misri, Girija Dhar, Sajida Zameer, Kaushalya Kaul and Usha Kak. She gave the impression that the 'militia' was essentially established to train women in self-defence, and every day the women used to gather at a specified time to learn how to use a .303 rifle, guns and grenades. General Cariappa and Colonel Sher Jung were the two names that emerged as those who had trained the women.

I asked Sukanya about the invasion of 1947; how she and other women would have heard of it, and what was being talked about at that time. 'We heard some news from Baramulla, that there were some people who were coming and we had to do something to stop them from entering Kashmir. Young men were involved; they were asked to come forward and enrol in an informal army. They were to be given training in arms; my brother was one of them. He also went to the front. We lost one of the boys from our neighbourhood; these young men were hardly trained at all. So then they tried to raise a women's militia. There was no pressure; we enrolled voluntarily, and then we were given training, and there were some lectures. We were prepared for a time that if the invaders came to Srinagar, how we would go about it.'

She continued: 'We heard that the Maharaja was running away with all his assets... Sheikh Abdullah was there, and then when the Maharaja left, the National Conference took over. Then of course, the songs and the marches...that is how it was! We also heard that the raiders were raping nuns, they were taking away women, and looting and burning... So all the Hindu women in my family and neighbourhood, along with my parents, moved to a Muslim locality, and we stayed there for two-three nights. They (the Muslims) said if anything had to happen, it would first happen to them! So we stayed with them till we heard there was no danger from the invaders any more. There was too much panic and tension all around.'

I asked her if she had actually seen the *kabailis*. She jumped with excitement like a little girl. 'Oh, yes! We heard that they had captured one (*kabaili*) and kept him in the prison... He had a long beard, and for us all this was very new and exciting. Also, he was in chains, which doubled the excitement.'

Coming to the lighter side of the women's training, Sukanya said, "There was a scarcity of salt at that time. Whenever we were tested (at the gun range) and did well, we were given salt and soap as reward! They used to keep targets in front of us, and we used to shoot. And a lot of us shot in the bull's eye...' I asked her how her family reacted to it. 'My parents were happy. However, my mother-in-law didn't like it very much. I would leave my children with my mother so that she would not be able to tell me anything! My husband was away studying, and I used to go for the training.'

From Sukanya's narration of the women's militia story, it was clear that most women became part of the corps with a burning desire to do something about the political unrest in Kashmir, and to be useful in some way. And when the air was rife with rumours that the invaders had come to loot land, property and women, the women's militia sprang up almost overnight. The militia never really got a chance to display their skill in the use of weaponry, as the invaders were taken care of by the Indian Army. However, the training and exposure certainly encouraged a tradition of women's education; the militia members subsequently took up positions as teachers and principals of women's schools and colleges in Kashmir. Sukanya herself was the principal of the Women's College in Srinagar until not long ago.

There was no future for the Self-Defence Corps, and it probably existed only for a few months. But it was a defining moment in the history of Kashmir, and definitely a defining moment in the lives of women who were a part of it. Later on – owing to the education, exposure and experience – these very same women went on to become pioneers in the field of education, heading schools and colleges; they broke new ground by taking up professions considered male territory, for example, in the field of medicine, as doctors and nurses; and paved the way for women's emancipation.

Over the years, I got an opportunity to meet some of the women Sukanya had mentioned, and we had rather animated conversations about the Kashmir of their times. Mahmooda Ahmed Ali Shah, now in her late 80s, had chosen to remain unmarried. A former head of the Government Women's College in Srinagar, she had been a Communist sympathizer, and had been active in the Congress party. She had also been a supporter of the National Conference since the 1940s. Sajida Zameer Ahmed was another strong supporter of women's rights. Krishna Misri was principal at the Srinagar Government Women's College, and was once a member of the Communist Party of India. Dr Girija Dhar had the first inter-religious marriage in Kashmir, to Dr Naseer Shah. Dr Dhar, a renowned doctor-surgeon, was the chairperson of Jammu and Kashmir State Women's Commission, but was forced to submit her resignation in February 2003 when a Congress–PDP coalition government took over the reins in the state.

Apart from training in the use of weapons, the self-defence corps members did the rounds of hospitals and met Indian soldiers who were wounded. They also went through the streets of Srinagar to distribute food and salt, as both were a rare commodity in those days. *People's Age*, a communist newspaper of those times, documented this movement on a regular basis, and even published photographs of women holding guns. One of the more famous photographs from those times is one in which Pandit Nehru is inspecting the militia.

The young woman who had earlier served us tea, Zooni, had been sitting with us all this while, listening with interest to Sukanya's anecdotal recounting. All I knew about her was that she was from Poonch, and had been living in Sukanya's house for a few years. I was pleasantly surprised when Sukanya told me that Zooni was planning a visit to Poonch, to her native village Kulali, and suggested I accompany her.

Zooni told me she had been part of a village defence committee – something that the government of India had advocated in the early '90s to combat militancy. VDCs comprised a group of villagers provided with weapons and trained in their use by the government. The twin villages of Kulali–Marrah in Surankote, the area Zooni hailed from, had the distinction of forming J&K's first all-women's VDC. This exercise was later repeated in district Reasi, but the novelty of Kulali–Marrah couldn't be trounced. Zooni recalled the incidents that led to the formation of the VDC, and I spent a couple of hours listening to her, making a few notes, before leaving Sukanya's house to prepare for travelling with Zooni the following day.

To get to Poonch district, Zooni and I first flew to Jammu, and then hopped onto a local bus. The ride thereon was full of bumps, amused looks from fellow-passengers, food and chai at local dhabas where the bus chose to halt, and breathtaking views, including those which displayed Border Roads Organization's signposts. One of them read: 'Love thy neighbour, but not on the road.'

A Kashmiri journalist-friend living in Jammu had requested a colleague of hers, Asad, to show us around in Poonch. Asad first took us to a point where 'India' and 'Pakistan' are on two sides of a river – the river being called Pulasi in India and Poonch Dariya in Pakistan. The colleague also took me to a point where the forward posts of the Indian and Pakistani armies – Bahadur and Durga, and Noorjahan and Mumtaz, respectively – were so close to each other that I wondered how the soldiers could resist greeting each other every morning; and how, during tense times, they could point a gun towards each other. In Jhalas, one of the villages in Poonch, the mobile networks played strange games. Indian service providers ceased to exist and humbly made way for Pakistani mobile networks – Ufone and Mobilink – among others. Near the Malti area, an elderly person shared with my companion how, in the good old days, he preferred to shop at Kota (across the border) than in Poonch town!

There was a massive earthquake here in 2005, causing widespread destruction on both sides of the border, especially along the Line of Control. India and Pakistan had then decided to open up five meeting points on the LoC to facilitate the meeting of families that were divided by the de facto border. At that point in time, it was considered a major confidence-building measure (CBM) between the two countries. Chakkan-da-Bagh, a little ahead of Poonch, was one of the more-celebrated and talked-about meeting points. At the same time, a token number of goods were exchanged at the meeting points. Pakistani *juttis* and *mojaris*, elaborately carved footwear for both men and women, were an instant hit in India. Pakistan seemed to have a huge appetite for vegetables, especially onions, grown on this side of the border, and lentils. However, like almost anything else between the two hostile neighbours, the elaborate ceremonies of the meeting points and trade diminished after reaching a crescendo.

In 2009, India and Pakistan were dwelling on making the LoC porous by opening another five points. It did seem like a significant step to revive the almost non-existent CBMs, but bureaucratic hurdles finally ensured that the opening of the meeting points would simply remain an attempted project on paper. Had it happened, it would have made a huge difference to those families divided between India and Pakistan when the LoC was drawn. There is no empirical evidence for this, but one had heard many a time that the LoC had run across houses as well, dividing them in two.

I tried to do a reality check and attempted to visit Chakkan-da-Bagh. Tedious paperwork and the fact that I, a non-Kashmiri, had been travelling the length and breadth of the land for many years now, ensured that the security personnel perceived me as a threat. I realized the torture the locals must go through to get a clearance to meet their kith and kin across the LoC. I wondered how many actually made it. Soon, we will lose a whole generation of people who would have lived before and just after the LoC was drawn.

After spending a day in Poonch, we took another local bus to Surankote, where my city-bred sensibilities had insisted I make arrangements to stay a night at the Army station before we went ahead in our journey to Kulali–Marrah. But once we reached Surankote, we were stationed at Draba for two days before we could travel further up the mountains to Kulali. We had to wait for the Sikh Regiment of 16 RR to carry out a road-opening ceremony (ROC). For the uninitiated, a ROC is an exercise which the Army conducts each morning (whenever possible, that is) with the assistance of bullet-proof and anti-blast paraphernalia to ensure that a particular route or road is clear of bombs and/or landmines or explosives. Sometimes this exercise is carried out with the help of locals who poke the ground with a long stick attached to a tiny device supposed to detect 'danger'. (Were they themselves not prone to blowing up if they were to step on a mine, I wondered?) Incidentally, the Rashtriya Rifles is one of the most high-powered special Army units created especially to fight insurgency in J&K. The RR's budget is separate from the defence budget of the country.

While we had no choice but to stay at Draba, we looked for ways to keep ourselves busy. Considering this was not a family posting, we only had Army jawans for company, and of course they were busy. Zooni and I had been cautioned against roaming around the Army camp as it was a highly sensitive zone, always under the enemy's watch, and at no cost could the two of us be 'seen'. We were on our best behaviour, and kept our conduct in strict accordance with the rules conveyed to us.

On day two of our confinement, however, the jawans took pity on us. They were going deep into the jungles to practice shooting, and asked if we would like to join them. Zooni and I went along with them excitedly. We walked for a few miles and reached a spot where the jungle had obviously been somewhat cleared to carry out such an exercise. The jawans set up several targets, and one by one started aiming and shooting at them. The commanding officer asked if we women were interested in trying it out too. This was something we couldn't resist, and immediately lined up to try our hand. One could never have imagined an AK-47 could be so heavy! Placing it on my right shoulder, I took aim and fired a shot. It felt like the earth under my feet had shuddered, and the noise of the bullet was deafening. Where the poor bullet ended up was anybody's guess. After several attempts to hit somewhere close to the target, I gave up, more due to the weight of the rifle than the disappointment of inaccuracy.

We were happy and excited at having tried something new and unusual, and when we returned to the camp, we were given the news that the ROC would be conducted in the wee hours of the following day. This meant that we could proceed to Kulali.

After much preparation, Zooni and I were 'escorted' uphill to Kulali, and amidst much fanfare, shown around the area. When I made it clear that I was going to park myself along with

Zooni in the village for the next couple of days to 'find out' things for myself, everyone was highly amused. One woman even told me she found it silly, and a waste of time, that I had come all the way from Delhi to Kulali just to speak to women VDC members, and all because they knew how to use guns and rifles!

Surankote *tehsil* has a fascinating story. Militancy came to the area in 1998 with Kashmiri militants who were friendly with the local civilians, who in turn supported them, particularly the women of the area, since the men usually stayed away from home for long stretches herding their cattle or for other work. Soon, the Kashmiri militants were overpowered by militants from the other side, largely from the LeT. They ill-treated the locals and ensured that no people from neighbouring areas such as Hill Kaka could stay there.

The dominant Gujjar population here had actively supported the Kashmiri militants. The women had happily provided for these young men, who promised them Azaadi. However, once the LeT took over, the area soon turned into a major operations base for the LeT, so much so that it was commonly referred to as 'mini-Pakistan'. The area was considered a 'liberated zone' till as late as 2002, and Pakistani flags on housetops and on vehicles were a common sight.

LeT insurgents often demanded food and shelter from the villagers, who complied. Soon, the demands turned more aggressive in nature, with the insurgents beginning to misbehave. Women were sexually harassed, and instances of molestation and rape became common. Men and children were made to work as porters without being remunerated. LeT cadre disrupted the functioning of the already limping government machinery and freely used the money, assets and resources of the local people. Many civilians were also killed.

The militants were able to do so primarily because the area was literally cut off from the rest of the world due to its difficult mountainous terrain, and also because most people, due to lack of exposure and education, had no reason whatsoever to disbelieve the militants. However, it is also true that the women were forced to provide for the militants for fear of their own lives and their dear ones.

In a complete turn of events, the locals, especially the women, began to openly resent the foreign mujahids. The villagers, both men and women, due to complete disillusionment with the militants, now joined hands with the Army and helped them 'clean' the area in one of the most massive operations carried out by Indian security forces in J&K: Operation Sarpvinash, in the year 2003.

The youth from the area, who were mostly working in Saudi Arabia, returned and decided to take charge of the situation. The turning point in this whole episode came when the younger brother of one of the village leaders was slain by insurgents for disobeying them. The locals approached the Army, and reported on the insurgents' base in the Hill Kaka range in the Kulali–Marrah area. The Army first built a road (there was none till then!), and carried out Operation Sarpvinash, a combing-out operation, from January to June 2003, with active support from the locals. The combined efforts of the locals and security forces resulted in the death of thirteen major terrorists and displaced several others. The Kulali–Marrah region was virtually cleansed of the foreign mujahids. Along with a formal all-men's defence committee, an all-women's VDC was also formed.

Of course, like most other events in J&K, this Army operation, too, is contested. There are allegations that Operation Sarpvinash was a major PR exercise done by the Army to cover up loopholes.

Roaming around Kulali–Marrah, mostly with Zooni and sometimes alone, I wasn't convinced about how the women's VDC came into existence, and I kept asking questions, sometimes silly ones. I was repeatedly told the narrative where there was an attack on a house and the woman of the house being all alone had no choice but to pick up her husband's rifle and start firing, setting an example for everyone else. The media started publicizing this incident so much that all the women in the area wanted to fire guns and make it to the headlines. Eventually, this resulted in the Kulali women's VDC.

According to another oft-repeated story, all the men in the area were forced to flee because the militants who had managed to escape during Operation Sarpvinash came back and threatened them. Everyday threats to their lives forced the men to go away to Saudi Arabia, and only the women were left in Kulali–Marrah, hence a women's VDC.

The 'official' version is the following: In the year 2004, some insurgents who had managed to flee during Operation Sarpvinash retaliated and killed about twenty villagers in Mohalla Teeyalikatha. This came to be known as the Teeyalikatha massacre. At the time, the VDC concept was just beginning to take roots, but this massacre changed the dynamics of a defence committee. So far the all-men's Kulali VDC had been going strong, but the Teeyalikatha massacre exposed the vulnerability of the women. It was then that the men decided to train their women in the use of arms. This resulted in J&K's first all-women's VDC, which began as an informal group of over 200 women trained in the use of arms. The VDC was formally recognized on 15 April 2004.

The story of Kulali–Marrah is not unique: it is the story of almost every village in insurgency-hit J&K, where locals first got carried away by the Azaadi sentiment, but later, disillusioned with the insurgents, decided to shift their stand. What is different here, however, is that Kulali–Marrah became one of the first to boast of an all-women's VDC. Even if it was a publicity stunt, even if it was just in name, the fact remains that it was, and is, one of a kind.

While it would not be incorrect to assume that almost every woman above the age of fifteen here could use weapons for self-defence, some of the daily issues of home and hearth they deal with make them no different from most women. Talking to different women during my wanderings about how they felt about using weapons, Munira Begum, an elderly woman, said: 'The gun made me feel that I have an equal status to that of my husband in our family.'

I was quite surprised, I have to admit, when I heard words like AK-47, SLR (Self-Loading Rifle), LMG (Light Machine Gun) and revolver roll off the tongues of the women here. Najma Akhtar told me: 'The Army trained the men in the village, and the men trained us in the use of weapons. I received my training informally with a few other women from my own village. As opposed to the men who carry their weapons with them all the time, we women keep our weapons at home, and take them out when we have to clean them or when there is a practice session. Though self-protection is the main motive behind learning how to use a weapon, when I first held a gun in my hands, the recurring thought in my head was that either I will die or I will kill the enemy. Earlier, militants used to take our men away, demand food and shelter and force us to have sex with them. If something like this happens now, I am sure I will be able to deal with the situation. I feel much more in control of the situation.'

Hospitality comes naturally to mountain people. When I started talking to Khursheeda Begum, she immediately invited me and Zooni over for a meal. She fed us a delicious meal, managing her ten-month-old wailing baby and talking of weapons and self-protection all at the same time. I knew women could multi-task, but this was unparalleled. She was of the view that 'guns and weapons are a way of life here. Whether we talk about it or not, the fact that every house has a weapon and every woman in the area can use those weapons means a lot to all of us. We feel secure as a community. Life has become peaceful now. We can breathe easy, eat and sleep without worrying. Our children can go to school, and study as long as they want to. The media highlighted our plight, as a result of which we have roads, electricity, schools, etc.'

Word spread around the village that there was a city-dweller eager to talk to the women. Ameera, a young woman of sixteen, stopped me while I was walking around and said, 'It was indispensable for us women to learn the use of weapons because in the absence of men, we have to protect ourselves.

Sometimes, people use their weapons for settling personal issues like land disputes. They even threaten each other on the basis of the weapons they possess. So that is the negative side of the training we have received. But otherwise, we are surer of ourselves than we were ever before.'

After meeting the women in Kulali, I wanted to explore adjoining areas in the hope of interacting with more women from the VDC. My guide, Lal Bhai, who, I was told, had had his moments of glory with militancy, couldn't believe this and tried hard to dissuade me. Amongst other things, he told me that the road didn't go beyond Kulali village, which, in effect, meant if Zooni and I wanted to go to the other areas, we would have to walk. He added politely, 'Walking in the mountains is no joke, and that too mountains which are infested with militants ...'

After a few minutes of arguments on his part and some assurances on ours, we found ourselves in the middle of a seven-member group – Zooni and I in the middle, four gun-toting Army jawans on all sides, and a not-very-pleased Lal Bhai leading us. We travelled on foot to cross two mountains, a few water bodies, and some deserted caves (which, Lal Bhai promptly informed us, used to serve as militant hideouts) to speak to a few more women. It took us approximately three hours one way, and I can still recall the amused looks on the women's faces when they were told about our reasons for visiting them. Later, I was also told that the four jawans had laid bets whether I would actually make the whole journey or decide to turn back halfway!

Sahba Bano, one of the women I met in the village, opened up to us after much reluctance and said, 'A few years ago, the

Army used to roam around during the day and the mujahids at night. We didn't know whom to support. Now, due to Operation Sarpvinash, there are virtually no militants in the area. But our men are away at work, and we are on our own. Even now, there are militant attacks at times; women didn't have a choice but to learn how to use weapons. As time went by, we got better at it. We realized we could live without fear. It was the feeling of "do or die". We don't know whether we will live for one hour or one year, but we live without fear.'

By now, we had been surrounded by a group of women, and questions were fired both ways. I got curious and asked what they did with their weapons when not using them. Alisha Bi replied: 'The weapon is usually kept at home, but when I go up to the forest to collect firewood or to graze the cattle, I always carry it with me. When I first held a gun in my hand, I forgot what fear is.' An image immediately conjured itself in my head: a pretty woman, a baby on her hip, a stick in one hand to manage her flock of sheep and an AK-47 hung in a carefree manner on her shoulder! She added: 'However, because we are women and we can use guns, we are aware that we have become targets of militants. But we are prepared for the worst.'

VDC members were not just trained in using weapons, but were also trained in minor tactics such as how to take positions and engage with insurgents. Each month, the Army took stock of the number of bullets, and firing tests were conducted to ensure the weapons were in a good condition. Nevertheless, the women complained that the weapons they possessed were not effective. Most weapons given to them were old and outdated. They feared that in case of a real attack, they may not be able to protect themselves. I asked if there had been any instances where they had to use their weapons, and they told me of two instances:

In November 2003, VDC members cordoned off three terrorists who had infiltrated their village. They managed to inform security forces, and killed one terrorist and injured the other two. In April 2004, terrorists entered Dophali, an adjoining area, burnt two houses and started firing at locals gathered to celebrate a wedding. But the VDC members fought them and saved many lives. It was after these two incidents of insurgency being successfully combated by women that the women's wing of the Kulali–Marrah VDC was formally recognized on 15 April 2004 by the commander of Rashtriya Rifles, Sector 6.

The women's VDC may be a media-savvy group now, considering the fact that many journalists have visited them, and they are aware of what they have achieved. The VDC itself may not be as functional or operational as it sounds, as we are in the post-militancy phase in J&K now. Despite all this, I remain in awe of the courage and enthusiasm of the women.

While I was at Surankote, I also decided to visit Noor-e-Chamb, a beautiful waterfall that merges with the river Surn. Named after the empress Noor Jehan, it is said that she used to come here for her daily baths, and a white spot just above the waterfall claims to have had a mirror stuck to it so that the royal lady could admire herself. On my way back to the Army base, I wondered if picking up arms for self-protection and for protecting the community would be something the queen would have approved of...

She surely would have been proud!

Zooni had been a silent but supportive companion all this while, accompanying me on my meandering walks and visits to different women in the villages. She had not said much, though. Each evening, when I had had my fill of conversations and chai with the village folk, we returned to Zooni's parental home to an evening filled with familial chit-chat, freshly cooked food, and more comfort and hospitality. There were several uncles, aunts and cousins, along with Zooni's parents, who shared the roof. Of course, the house was as much theirs as that of their cattle, who roamed in and out freely. The scene each day was that of domestic bliss. It was no surprise then that the family didn't even blink an eyelid when Zooni announced I was going to be their guest for a few days.

One evening, Zooni decided to open up to me. As we were returning home after the usual walk through the village, she suggested we stop at a cliff overlooking the beautiful meadows of Surankote. It had been a bright and warm day, and the sun was about to move on to other pastures, turning the sky into a mass of golden-pink light. I sensed Zooni's willingness to talk, and asked if she had ever considered the option of learning how to use weapons.

'The wave took everyone along in its tide,' she told me. 'Of course, I, too, was inspired to learn how to shoot. But I got carried away in trying to explore my own Azaadi.' I prodded her some more and out came the whole story.

When the entire area of Kulali–Marrah had been raging against the atrocities of the militants, young Zooni fell in love with Khalid, a militant, who brought along with him uncertainty, danger, adventure and risk. Soon, everyone in the village knew of this little story on the sidelines of the bigger drama of militancy and women learning self-defence techniques. It reached a point where Zooni's family was being threatened, on one hand by the militants, and on the other, by the villagers. In what seemed like a typical love saga, the young lovers didn't know whether to follow their hearts or to follow 'advice' from elders. Each was exploring their own Azaadi, trying to break free from norms. The couple finally decided to run away from the village, uncertain of what to do next, but sure of being with each other and sticking it out together.

Of course, it was not to be. Just a couple of days before the big event in their lives, Khalid apparently went 'missing'. Zooni could not ask anybody to find out anything, and her own attempts to locate him were futile. She heard rumours that his organization had 'moved' him from the area to prevent him from getting distracted from the 'cause'. There was nothing Zooni could do about it. She did not want to stay in the village any longer and her family was only too keen to send her away. It was at this time that Sukanya Parashar came into the picture.

Sukanya was known to the villagers as she used to visit Kulali–Marrah at the Army's behest to inspire the women. She was an example to them, owing to her own tryst with the 1947 militia. She came to Zooni's rescue when she realized the girl wanted to move away from her family and village, and the family was happy to give her charge of Zooni.

Those few days spent in Kulali–Marrah taught me some important lessons in survival tactics. I had newfound respect for people living in areas so remote and inaccessible that it took massacres and human rights violations of the worst kind for authorities to take cognizance and construct something as basic as a road. On my way back to the valley from Kulali, I wondered if the United Nations Security Council Resolution (UNSCR) 1325 would acknowledge the women of Kulali–Marrah. UNSCR 1325 remains the first resolution passed by the Security Council to specifically address the impact of war on women, and women's contributions to conflict resolution and sustainable peace. The resolution reaffirms the important role of women in the prevention and resolution of conflicts, peace negotiations, peace-building, peacekeeping, humanitarian responses and in post-conflict reconstruction efforts.

When I first visited Kashmir in May 2003 and wanted to live in a houseboat, Hussain had promptly taken me to Rasheed sa'ab, who owned an old but magnificent houseboat on the Nagin lake. Rasheed has, over the years, become a friend, and very warmly extends his hospitality every time I visit Srinagar. It was he who was instrumental in steering my thoughts towards what I was attempting to do.

I had, for years, been researching on the various aspects of the Kashmir conflict with a conscious focus towards the female gender. As in most other facets of life, the conflict and the varied theories emerging thereof lacked women's voices. I felt the need to know more about the state through its women. And it was largely because of Rasheed sa'ab that I decided to plan a women's workshop, more so to expand my horizons.

In order to fully comprehend Kashmir's desire for Azaadi, I had to get the women's point of view. And it had to be more than simply understanding women to be victims of the conflict. True, they were victims; yet, at the same time, they were also survivors. I had to find those few voices who had dared to speak, to rebel and to create their own space. The workshop, which I had named 'Women's Voices from J&K', was going to be an attempt to bring together women from different walks of life, and would include women living near the border areas – areas considered inaccessible and remote for various reasons, 'security' being one of them.

I had mapped the media scene in J&K in 2005. The media initiative had sought to constructively engage local journalists, develop a network with journalists in the process and form a core group from this association that could serve as an advisory body to help journalists in the two main cities of Jammu and Srinagar to narrow down their own divides and work together towards meaningful reporting from the conflict zone of Jammu and Kashmir. During my interaction with the journalists, I couldn't help observing the stark difference in opinion between journalists in Jammu and those in Kashmir. The former did not hesitate to make it very clear that Srinagar, and its media, did not want to let go of the conflict. I felt the Jammu journalists were resenting the fact that even though Jammu and its adjoining areas had also been severely affected by the conflict, the valley got the maximum attention in terms of headlines and news coverage. Meanwhile, journalists from the valley were of the opinion that the major part of the turmoil in the Jammu region was mostly brought about by the internal conflict between Jammu, Kashmir and Ladakh, and it had very little to do with the larger Kashmir conflict.

However, the one area where I noticed a similarity in both places was increased reportage on human interest stories, and covering social and developmental issues rather than conflict-related stories. There was a conscious shift in focus from covering militancy, the security situation, and the daily toll of violence to covering the healthcare sector (absolute lack of psychiatric care, condition of hospitals, unregulated medicines and service providers), lack of public awareness regarding government provisions, ecological impacts of tourism, and efforts to maintain the Dal Lake. This was a very welcome change, a change that took place from the year 2006 onwards.

The focus of the media, nevertheless, kept coming back to the conflict, and understandably so, given the trajectory of events in Kashmir. Some journalist friends shared with me that while they realised it was essential the media did not sensationalize any event or incident, unfortunately, they had to do so to maintain their readership. They agreed that the media was responsible for the conflict being blown out of proportion. After politicians, journalists had created divides and given rise to conflicts, since it was their 'bread and butter', with their biased reportage.

There were many women columnists in Kashmir before the unrest began. However, after the conflict and its 'Islamist turn', women began to avoid professional engagements such as journalism. Some local editors on their part were not willing to take on women reporters, keeping in mind the directives of some insurgent groups. This added to the 'masculinization' of the media and, in turn, the Kashmiri voice, after 1989. The situation has changed drastically now, and there are many women journalists both in Jammu and Srinagar. A lot of women are also enrolling in media-oriented studies such as the Mass Communications degree at the University of Kashmir.

Coming back to the workshop: 'Women's Voices from J&K' was to follow a similar trajectory. My approach was to travel widely, and identify women who would collaborate with me in different ways. Along the way, I was to try and get groups of two to three women to meet with each other and discuss their own viewpoints related to the conflict. What I was looking forward to the most was how each of these women would define their own Azaadi, their personal liberation, which would be a mix of domestic as well as public life. At the end of my travels towards this initiative, I would hopefully have identified a group of five to seven women, from varied age groups, who would then come together and explore further the term 'Azaadi' in the context of Kashmir.

'The term "migration camp" cannot be used in the case of Kashmiri Pandits who were compelled to flee the valley, and who were "relocated" in government-provided set-ups on the outskirts of Jammu city or elsewhere. The term "refugee camp" is more appropriate.' Thus started my conversation with Ananya Bhat when I went to meet her at the guesthouse she was staying at during the promotional tour of her collection of stories, *In the Desire for Freedom*.

I couldn't help but agree. Migration refers to a periodic shift from one region to another, and indicates a willing change in position. The same cannot be said of Kashmiri Pandits who were forced, by a series of planned and executed events, to make a mass exit from the valley. And one could only refer to them as refugees – someone who flees for safety reasons, especially to a foreign land, during a time of political upheaval.

A Kashmiri Pandit in her early thirties, Ananya had left the valley when she was barely six or seven, during the mass exodus of Kashmiri Pandits. Growing up in the Purkhoo migrant camp on the outskirts of Jammu city, her childhood was lived in an atmosphere of constant fear, stress, nostalgia and anxiety, and she was largely raised on an overdose of hatred for everything to do with Kashmiri Muslims, for no fault of hers, or theirs. She had memories of growing up in the midst of utter chaos, owing to threatening phone calls at her home, neighbours banging on the door in the middle of the night to huddle together for safety, announcements on the loudspeaker 'recommending' Pandits to leave the valley or face the consequences, reports of Pandit women being harassed when they stepped out on the roads, the sudden need for the women to wear bindis on their foreheads…

One fine day – rather, at night – the chaos came to an end. The little girl found herself hauled into a truck along with her older brother, parents, grandmother and several of their neighbours along with their families. In the middle of the night, despite everyone advised to be as discreet and silent as possible, it seemed to the children that they were venturing out on one big adventure trip. However, what awaited them in Purkhoo on the outskirts of Jammu was quite an anti-climax.

After living in the 'migrant camps' for more than two decades, the old died in the hope of returning to their houses, their lands, their neighbourhood, their apple orchards – i.e., the lives they were used to and the only lives they knew. Meanwhile, the young became hostile, unreceptive, unfriendly and angry. They grew up to become aggressive old people living in the constant shadow of their uprooted and displaced past. It was worse for the children. They learnt not the stories of good triumphing over evil, but rather of evil slowly creeping into people's lives from their backyards and taking over an entire community's harmonious coexistence. One such child was Ananya Bhat.

Being used to living in a large, open house with a garden to boast of, it was a task to get used to the cramped, ugly and unhygienic conditions of Purkhoo. Though food had never been a priority for Ananya, she could sense that there was never enough for the six of them huddled in their tent. What was more difficult to fathom was everyone sticking together at all times – be it groups of men, women, elders, even family members. Everyone simply seemed to be sitting around all day, almost in fear of losing sight of one another. The child's mind perceived it as abnormal; what it could not perceive, however, was the reason for it – there was simply nothing else to do! What could multitudes of people – people who had been picked up from a place where everything was familiar and put in another where everything was just the opposite – do anyway?

Gradually, Ananya saw that she and her community were without roots. The 'stories' of trauma and anguish that she had witnessed since the night of the exodus slowly and painfully became real and drove home the point. Amongst all, one in particular remains etched on her mind.

When in the valley, Ananya went to the posh private school in the neighbourhood. She was adored by most of her classmates and teachers. Mrs Kaul, her English teacher, in particular, was extremely fond of her and went out of her way to take care of her, especially since the student and teacher lived in the same neighbourhood. When trouble began to brew, the Bhats and the Kauls got warning signals and threat calls around the same time. Each evening would bring with it a fresh incident of trauma in the form of some woman in the neighbourhood being harassed, or some neighbour being held captive for a few hours, tortured, then released to tell the tale. According to the grapevine, Mrs Kaul had borne no children, because of which her husband had 'abandoned' her. She lived with her aged and frail mother. A few distant relatives would come by once in a while to check on the two women, but they had no family to speak of. The neighbourhood served as their support structure in their hour of need, and they had grown used to the idea of a lonely existence. The continuous accumulation of stress, anxiety and anguish over the past several months had not helped the older woman's medical condition, especially her weak heart, at all. And then, when the D-day finally arrived, it crept up on them very quietly, on tiptoe, and without a warning. The elders in the neighbourhood sat huddled together at the Bhats' residence, unable to decide what to do. Extremist forces had given them an ultimatum to leave the valley. Though the Pandits had been hearing such ultimatums over the months, the tension in the air that day was too thick to ignore. Suddenly, there was a fresh burst of rioting in the area, and amidst tear gas shells, vehicles on fire, violent abuses, and frantic appeals for help from families around, they decided to leave town. Though it was a collective decision, somebody had to inform every individual household in the locality. While some got around to doing that, others were left to arrange for the escape, without knowing exactly where to go, and how.

Ananya's father was sent to Mrs Kaul's house to tell the women to prepare to leave immediately. The older of the two women was unable to deal with the shock of this news, and succumbed to a heart attack. Seeking help was impossible on two accounts: one, going out to arrange for medical facilities was impractical; and two, Mrs Kaul's mother chose a hasty exit to unite with her Maker rather than exit to an unknown, uncertain future. Mrs Kaul and Mr Bhat, and everyone else, when they found out about the incident couldn't help observe the untimely death. The question that faced them now was: what to do about it? Arranging to perform the last rites was impossible. So while some elders of the community chose to inform everyone of their mass exodus the same evening and some others arranged for it to happen, it was left to the senior-most members to take a call on the dead body which lay amidst them.

For lack of an alternative, the old woman's body was hauled on to the same truck which was to carry some of the families and their most basic necessities of life to an unknown place. There were very few things that Ananya remembered as clearly, categorically and vividly as travelling on the same truck as a dead body. The ensuing silence spoke volumes. What happened next, how the body was cremated, and how and where the community decided to set up base were all irrelevant in the enormity of what had just happened.

During my conversations with Ananya, it was obvious that the bitterness had remained, and had made her and others her age grow far beyond their years. It probably would have made sense, for posterity's sake, to ask her questions like what were the reactions of their Muslim neighbours; how did they indicate, if at all they did, that the Pandits should leave? Were the reactions and behaviour of the men different than the women?

Growing up in Purkhoo left an indelible mark on Ananya as it did on the thousands of others in the numerous 'migrant camps' for Kashmiri Pandits – Misriwala, Nagrota, Muthi, etc. Meanwhile, in a painfully protracted process spanning more than a decade-and-a-half, Suresh Bhat, Ananya's father, was able to set up a small business venture and move his family out of the camp. His children were able to receive education in a reasonably decent school; there was enough food in the house and for the occasional guests and friends too; his parents, though they kept yearning for the valley to which they would never return, died under their own roof; and his wife could afford to buy enough clothes not just for the children but also for herself.

After she finished school, Ananya managed to travel abroad on a series of scholarships, and did not return to Jammu for almost five years. When she came back with her ideas to elevate the status of her people in the light of their sufferings, she found herself a complete misfit in the Pandit community, and was almost ostracized. The new sensibilities that Ananya had acquired as a result of the education and exposure she had received deemed it difficult to accept the way the women of the community were treated. The men, full of disappointment because nothing seemed to be working out or working in their favour, had no other outlet for their frustration except their womenfolk. Making tough conditions even worse for the women by controlling every little thing they did – from buying groceries to the way they dressed – the men dictated everything. Obviously, the women were miserable. Seeing this, Ananya would bring together groups of women and counsel them. The community viewed it as an open rebellion; word spread around that Ananya was encouraging and even teaching the women how to rebel. It was with great difficulty, and over a long period of time, that this point of view about her changed, and she found acceptance, first at home, and then in the neighbourhood.

Once she settled back amidst all the confusion, and there was some semblance of a patch-up with the family and community, Ananya got down to compiling a collection of short stories, each depicting a Pandit woman and her fleeing from the valley, whether out of choice or forcibly. Each story was an account of the woman's personalized journey from captivity to freedom, for better or worse. The subject being cyclic, she managed to find a suitable publisher. The book was a huge success, and more importantly, a cathartic experience for the writer. Moved by the whole experience and the response that came about with the publication of the book, Ananya decided to build a public platform for women through a women's magazine she chose to call *Voices*. It was this platform that I was hoping to gain access to and use as a medium for bringing together the women of J&K.

Ananya and I decided to visit some of the migrant camps in Jammu. I was hoping to gain access to the lives of the women in the camps through Ananya; she and her family had lived in the camp for many years, and she had come back to the camp after her meanderings around the world. Of course she had faced stiff opposition at first, but later came acceptance, and it bore fruit in the form of women opening up to her like the dam gates of a flooded river being opened.

Spending time with Ananya made one thing very clear to me: she had no patience for mediocrity. Having been through turbulence ever since she could remember, she had no soft corners for anyone who chose to indulge in self pity. Her mantra was basic: Figure out a way to fight with your troubles, or else, don't complain.

At Misriwala camp, I was surprised at the ease and comfort with which she weaved her way through the narrow bylanes and huts. We stopped in front of a door, and she knocked. I had neither been prepared for nor warned about the story that was about to come my way. We were greeted by an elegant and beautiful woman whose face bore the marks of time and turmoil. Despite the difference in age, Sarla and Ananya met like two long-lost friends. I was ushered into a sparsely furnished room, the ceiling of which was low enough for me to raise my hand and touch it.

During the time of the exodus, as the news spread like wildfire that the Pandits either had to leave the valley or die, Sarla had been married for a few years and had a two-year-old daughter, Kamlesh. The decision to leave was made at the last minute, and it was a mad rush to put together only the absolutely necessary belongings. Neighbours gathered outside their respective houses, because everyone was to leave together and nobody could afford to not be part of the group, and the men made the final arrangements to exit the place they had all known as 'home'.

Kamlesh suddenly realized she had left her dolls behind. She expressed her concern to Sarla, who chided the child. She was too caught up in the whirlpool of her individual as well as the community's emotions at what was happening, not realizing the simplicity and innocence of the child's worries. Making use of the chaos and confusion all around, Kamlesh slipped away from her mother's side to run to her house and retrieve her dolls. The child was too naive to understand the implications of her actions.

In a fresh burst of violence, a mob had set a few houses in the neighbourhood on fire and was going around creating havoc. By the time Sarla realized Kamlesh's absence, the fire had spread uncontrollably. In sheer panic, she looked around for her child. A frantic search of the neighbourhood proved futile. In a sudden moment of agony, she realized where her daughter had gone. Sarla raced towards her house, only to find it blazing with the flames of fire doused in communal hatred and violence. There was no way she could go inside, and there was no way to find out if her child was trapped. The pressure was building to leave immediately. In the craziness of the hour, it was decided that Sarla's husband would stay behind and look for the child, and the two of them would join the next group of Pandits leaving the valley the following day. Sarla was given no option but to leave right then.

As the refugees were being assembled on the outskirts of Jammu and the local administration tried to create some method in the madness of the riots, Sarla's hopes of being reunited with her husband and child were renewed with each fresh batch of refugees. But each passing day brought no news, only despair. After a week of torturous waiting, Sarla found out about their deaths.

I did not have the heart to ask Sarla if she knew the details of how it happened; if her husband and child were given a decent cremation; if the news of their death was a certainty. All these questions seemed futile after all these years. I also could not gather the courage to ask her how she managed on her own in the aftermath of these two colossal tragedies. Ananya filled in the gaps by saying Sarla took on the responsibility of mentoring and tutoring as many children in her migrant camp as she possibly could. In return, their parents ensured Sarla had food to eat and clothes to wear.

In a community barely able to keep pace with the rollercoaster of events, money and livelihood seemed like two distinct jokes. Many years after these events happened, the community must have thought about them in retrospect and wondered if the outcomes would have been different had they dealt with things differently. What we usually forget in times of retrospection is that in the moment of despair, what was done was probably the best that could have been done.

But who could clear the conscience of a mother who must have blamed herself every single minute of her life for letting her child slip away? Who would be able to explain to a woman that she was in no way responsible for her husband having to stay behind to look for their daughter?

Over the course of the next few weeks, I visited three different migrant camps, other than Misriwala, on the outskirts of Jammu – Purkhoo, Muthi and Jagati – with Ananya and two of her friends. All the narratives I heard were, naturally, loaded with painful memories; regret and remorse at things that had not been in their control. While it was clear that Ananya and her friends Sanjay and Rekha visited the camps regularly, and were familiar with the lives of most of the people there, I felt like an intruder. I had no right to expect the people to re-visit their past simply because I wanted to know what had happened. I had spoken to many people – women, men and children. I had heard their woes; they had made the time to sit and talk to me. But did I have any solutions for their problems? What right did I have to go and demand they share their lives with me?

I told Veena, one of the young women I met in a camp, that all her aches and pains were due to lack of nourishment. I said, 'You must maintain a balanced diet.' Her answer was simple: 'When there is never enough food, you think I could be worried about balancing it...'

Was I promoting 'disaster tourism'? In the course of identifying women for my women's initiative workshop, was I becoming indifferent towards the fragility of the issue; the trauma that the women had undergone in the past, and were forced to revisit because of me? I had no answer.

# Narcissus & Lotus

*What the books taught me, I've practised.*
*What they didn't teach me, I've taught myself.*
*I've gone into the forest and wrestled with the lion.*
*I didn't get this far by teaching one thing and doing another.*[36]

The setting was idyllic, with pretty Kashmiri women everywhere, cattle roaming around in all directions, lush green chinar leaves all around, a stream of cool, sweet water flowing at one side. Yet, there was a palpable unrest among the group of women with whom I was conducting a workshop on 'trauma-healing and reconciliation'.

I was unable to figure out the tension while the women went through the rituals of the workshop half-heartedly. We broke up for lunch and I wandered across to the stream in true Bollywood-style to wash my hands and feel the coolness of the water. As I sat there, one of the women from the group came rushing towards me in what seemed like a state of panic. She urged me to return to the building where the workshop was going on. I asked her what the matter was, and after much cajoling, she said there were *mehmaan* (guests) in the village. I was amused, and asked her why I needed to go back simply because there were visitors in the village. In fact, I suggested to her to invite the visitors to join the workshop! She smirked at my ignorance, and almost dragged me back inside. Then came the moment of truth: men from the HM were referred to as *mehmaan*, while those from the LeT were deemed to be *khaas* (special) *mehmaan*.

We decided to conclude the workshop then and there. It was one thing to talk about 'peace', 'reconciliation' and 'trauma-healing', and quite another to know we were in the vicinity of 'guests'! At this point, I woke up with a start from my dream, as I had several times before. Always the same dream, the same surroundings and set-up, the same feeling of disturbed calmness...

During my first interaction with a group of women labelled 'half-widows' – women whose husbands are not officially declared dead, but termed 'missing' – from Dardpora in 2003, it was difficult for me to fathom how a man could simply 'disappear'. Of course things have become clearer now, but that first time was numbing, to say the least.

Amongst this group of women from Dardpora was Rafiqa, a woman in her mid-twenties, who looked stunningly beautiful in her salwar-kameez detailed with Kashmiri embroidery. I can recall my conversation, with an eager-to-talk Rafiqa, to the last detail even to this day. Her husband had been picked up, presumably by the security forces, and taken away, never to return. She was left behind with two children, both below five, and nothing but memories of her husband. Her in-laws turned her out from their house, and other men from the village harassed her day and night. She did not want to burden her parents, but had no choice but to return to their house. Amongst other things, her biggest regret was that she and her husband only managed to have two children before he 'disappeared'. She didn't want to 'retire' so soon. She had wanted many more children. I wasn't sure if it was appropriate to suggest a second marriage to Rafiqa. The Indian government does not provide any relief to half-widows before seven years from the date of the 'disappearance' of their men, and if the women choose to re-marry before those seven years, they are not entitled to any official relief or assistance whatsoever. Until recently, the government had provided relief only to a few hundred half-widows.

For Rafiqa, as for most women of Kashmir, the conflict has been doubly fatal, as they haven't just borne the wrath of the conflict but have also been treated as objects of use and amusement, both by militants and Indian security forces. I was meeting her again, after a gap of many years, during my current visit to the valley. In trying to find her own Azaadi, she had fought the battle of survival ferociously. The journey had been long and painful. She had visibly aged, but was still stunning, and in control of life. It was difficult to imagine how she must have toiled and fretted over re-building it bit by bit. She seemed reluctant to talk about it. I decided to go with Rafiqa to her village, Dardpora.

Dardpora, the 'village of widows' in Kupwara, is nestled in the mountains and is very close to the LoC. Its name comes from the Dardi tribe which inhabits the village. Ironically, it also symbolizes *dard,* or the pain and suffering, that the women here undergo. Even though I had been to the village before, going with Rafiqa was a different experience. She had been born and brought up in Dardpora, and had been married to a man from the same village, Suleiman.

In the early 1990s, when militancy was just setting foot in Kashmir, three militant groups – Al Barq (mostly comprising Gujjars), HM, and the Kashmir Liberation Force – became operational in the area. A fratricidal war between the three groups and clashes with security forces claimed most of the men in this village. Prior to that, the hostility between the two prevalent communities – Gujjars and Kashmiris – had taken the lives of many male members. As a tragic and sad after-effect, those who were left in the village were mostly women and children, women whose men had either died or had gone 'missing'. Women whose husbands went 'missing' began to be known as 'half-widows'.

Hussain drove the two of us up to Dardpora. It had snowed the previous day, an unusual phenomenon for the month of November. After four hours of a journey full of twists and turns on long, winding roads through thick forests of unparalleled scenic beauty, we reached the outskirts of the village, beyond which we had to make our way on foot. Hussain wasn't too happy about this, but once he realized Rafiqa and I wouldn't be deterred, he reluctantly parked his vehicle and followed us – a gesture which deeply touched me. His job was simply to take me to places, not to worry about my whereabouts and safety. But over the years, Hussain had donned the mantle of being my guardian angel in Kashmir: ensuring I ate my meals, called home and informed my family of my well-being, and didn't get too 'adventurous'.

Rafiqa took us to her parents' house, where she had been living along with her two children after her husband went 'missing' and the in-laws turned hostile. Having spent some time talking to Rafiqa's mother and sharing tit-bits of information about my work in general, I expressed a desire to walk through the village. '*Yahan par charon taraf dushman hai. Kisi par bharosa nahi kiya ja sakta,*' the elderly woman told me. Everyone here is an enemy. No one can be trusted...

Hussain made his exit at this point, and Rafiqa and I spent the better part of the afternoon walking aimlessly around lower Dardpora exchanging pleasantries with the village folk. Most of the widows in the village were very young, between twenty-one and forty-five years. Most had large families, with school-going children to support. Earlier, Gujjar women would go to the jungles to chop firewood that they would then sell, and Kashmiri women would cultivate the land or earn a meagre income from handicraft orders. Now, widowhood had become the dominant marker for these women. They were harassed by security forces and militants alike, not to mention the daily struggle of having to fend for themselves and their children.

It came to light that there was once a time when there was not a single house in Dardpora that did not house militants. Women had a choice between willingly marrying the militants or being forcefully carried away. After the men/militants were killed, the women did not remarry because of their children. They also said that nobody wanted a woman with children from a previous marriage. Since livelihood means were scarce, and it was only women left behind in Dardpora, prostitution could not be ruled out. I had to be very gentle about asking them if they had been harassed by security forces or government officials. They denied that this was happening, and indicated that as they were now liberated from all men, issues of rape, battering and assault were no longer relevant.

The basis of my interactions with the women in Dardpora, as anywhere else in Kashmir, had to be trust, which I had to work upon. Rafiqa was going to help me with that. My first interaction with the Dardpora women had taken place in Srinagar many years before. We had invited a group of twenty women from the village to stay with us for a two-day 'trauma healing and reconciliation' workshop. For the Dardpora women, it was strange to be away from the village, stranger still that they didn't have to look after the house, cook, clean and manage the children. What was worse was that there was someone else who was happy to cook for them and feed them! A shikara ride on the Dal lake, which we all take for granted as part of the deal when visiting Kashmir, put these women in a state of utter confusion and deep, far-away thoughts.

In trauma healing, symbolism plays a crucial role. During the course of the workshop, it was important for us as the team conducting the workshop to establish an act of symbolism that we could relate to as ours, as belonging especially to our group – the Dardpora women and the team from Delhi. We tried to get the group to do several things: sing, draw, do an exercise wherein we divided the group in pairs. Nothing seemed to be working. It was an intense and extremely challenging experience to even get the women to talk. All they wanted was some money, and be allowed to go back home to their children. 'Caring and sharing' was a concept alien to them, and they didn't think much of 'talking'.

Amongst other things, conflict teaches people survival tactics. An important part of that is to be able to say things the other party wants to hear. So the Dardpora women said the 'right' things which were meant to move us women from Delhi to tears; however, our training and experience warned us that not everything we were told was true.

After day one of the workshop, as I was talking to the group during dinner, one of the women took me aside, and putting my hand inside her *pheran,* told me she had no breasts as the militants had simply chopped them off! My instant reaction was denial. How could this be possible? However, it was.

In Kashmir, thousands of women are going through an identity crisis owing to the phenomenon of enforced disappearances, which leads them to the status of half-widows. For such women, each day begins with the hope of their men returning, and ends in despair. While officials put the number of enforced disappearances between 1,000 and 3,000, according to human rights activists at least 10,000 people have been made to disappear by state agencies, mostly by armed personnel, in the last twenty years. Many of them were young men, and their disappearance has left behind 2,000 to 2,500 half-widows.[37]

The official version on these disappearances is bleak. Most men are either taken away under cover of darkness, or picked up from somewhere where nobody can identify the person or even know the location from where the disappearance took place. The ones taken away for questioning on the pretext of a 'crime' or 'violent incident' are said to be kept under tight security where neither their families are allowed to meet them nor are they given any legal assistance. Year after year, they remain missing, and the government does not say where they are.

Most half-widows are women from lower-income families and mostly dependent on their husbands. During the seven-year waiting period, the women's rights to their husbands' property are often threatened. As is common, there is little or no support from the in-laws. Even after the completion of seven years from the date of disappearance, the women get a meagre amount of money for their sustenance. Half-widows have no recourse to justice or provision of aid, especially in the form of employment. Many NGOs, both local and national, have opened schools for these women where they are taught stitching and embroidery, and at times, given sewing machines. This is hardly enough or practical to help the women out of their plight.

When I had visited Dardpora after the two-day workshop in May 2003, there was a certain sadness that hung around the place like a gloomy cover. It seemed like life itself was dishevelled, unkempt and lost. For the inhabitants of Dardpora, mostly women, their days revolved around a few fruit trees, farming land where they cultivated some rice, and perhaps a small income from a room or two given out on rent. There was one school with only one old man acting as both schoolmaster and mentor for the fifteen-odd children of all age groups who came there.

When I visited Dardpora the second time, Master sahib was happy to see me again, this time with Rafiqa. During a long chat over a cup of *noon chai*, the salty tea for which I had finally acquired a taste, he told me how it was important for the women of Dardpora to have exposure to the outside world and interact with people beyond the village.

When word spread that the 'madam' from Delhi had come, some of the women from the village came to greet me. I was delighted that two of them were from the same group I had met earlier in Srinagar, and what's more, they even remembered me! After exchanging polite banter, I was ushered into one of their homes and offered tea and blankets to keep me warm. On the way, I noticed a small stitching school. There wasn't much progress in the village in terms of development, but the gloomy cover had certainly lifted. Even the school premises looked impressive and had an air of self-importance about it.

However, not much seemed to have changed in the lives of the women. They were still waiting to hear news of their missing men; reports still emanated of them being tortured by militants and security forces for the same reasons; they continued to wonder where their next meal would come from.

Rafiqa and I made our way back to her parents' house, and by now, her father and her two children were also home. While the mother and daughter got busy with preparing the evening meal, and the father entertained a group of his friends, I tried to talk to the children. They responded by bringing their school bags and displaying their books. I asked them if they liked school and what they did there. 'We study, and we play terrorist-terrorist, and sometimes when one of us can't be found by the others, that child is considered "missing".' The ease with which the children said this sent a chill down my spine.

Almost all children in Kashmir have been affected by the conflict – while some are the children of insurgents, there are others who have lost their parents to the insurgency. Some have been physically affected by the conflict, a victim in a violent incident; others have been badly affected psychologically. While the children in far-flung areas like Dardpora undergo formal education courtesy NGOs and some government infrastructure, there is little or no exposure to the outside world, particularly due to lack of interaction with people outside their own area.

In such a situation, how do children cope with the trauma of conflict? The answer was in front of my eyes: they do so by playing games like 'terrorist-terrorist'. I have often wondered how their innocent minds address the issues of fear, hatred, anger, rebellion, trauma, disaster, compassion, reconciliation etc. Do they ever get healed? How do the children react to being identified as 'victims', and how does it affect their growing up? How does conflict affect their interactions with each other, particularly during extra-curricular activities? Again, I had no answers.

I mentioned this to Rafiqa as soon as we had all retired for the day after a delicious meal of *haq* (locally grown spinach) and rice with *yakhni* (meat cooked with spices and curd). She was not surprised. According to her, it was not just hers but most children of Kashmir who played such games and spoke in this manner. She also mentioned another 'favourite' game Kashmiri children played: during firing, which is a common feature of everyday life here, children derived thrills by trying to establish whether it was the sound of rifles, AK-47s or some other gun!

I only had to slightly encourage Rafiqa to tell me her story, and she began telling me what had transpired in her life. Suleiman and Rafiqa had gotten married in the village ten-odd years ago and had begun their family almost immediately. Suleiman was a porter, and there was a rumour that he, along with twenty other men from the village, was involved with a militant group and helped them in various ways. Rumour also had it that since Kupwara was very close to the LoC, one of the routes that militants on both sides used to cross the border was through Dardpora.

Rafiqa said Suleiman had been warned a couple of times by the armed forces that he was under watch and his daily activities were being closely followed. One day, Suleiman left home in the wee hours of the morning, even before the darkness of the night had given way to the sunrise. He told Rafiqa he was going for work, and she knew better than to ask more.

Suleiman met up with his acquaintances in the deep cover of the forest, and together they set out even deeper. They were to meet up with foreign militants and bring them to safety. However, security forces had come to know of this movement, and had been keeping watch for a few days now. Suleiman was oblivious to this. Suspecting nothing, the group moved on. Soon enough, there was an ambush; the security forces had formed a ring around them. Caught unawares, the militants fared badly in the clash, and most of them succumbed to the bullets. The few who survived tried to run away into hiding.

When Rafiqa heard persistent banging on her door, and that too only a few hours after her husband had left, she immediately sensed trouble. She opened the door to find a badly injured Suleiman almost collapsing outside the house. She got him inside, and helped him to bed. He refused her offer to bring Khan Chacha who acted as the village doctor, even though he had no medical background. But once Suleiman lost consciousness, Rafiqa immediately went and fetched the old man. She wasn't very happy to note Chacha's expression on examining her husband.

After treating four bullet injuries with whatever could be used as equipment from within the house, Khan Chacha administered Suleiman some local herbs as medicine, and told Rafiqa in no uncertain terms that his chances of survival were bleak. He suggested that if and when Suleiman recovered from unconsciousness, he should not be allowed to move at all. With a promise of coming back to check on Suleiman, he left. Rafiqa was lost. She knew that word would soon spread around the village about Suleiman and his injuries, even though Chacha would not be the one doing the talking. She didn't know what to say to her children and Suleiman's parents. However, she knew she had to move her husband away from the house because the security forces would come looking for him any minute. This she did with the help of Chacha and some other elders;

Suleiman was moved to an abandoned and well-hidden cave in the forest.

In a few weeks' time, when Suleiman had regained and lost consciousness several times before finally coming about, and when the whole village including his parents and children knew what had transpired, there was an air of discomfort all around. Suleiman insisted on going deeper into the forest to make contact with the foreign militants to find out what had happened that morning. Rafiqa and the others could not stop him. The inevitable happened: Suleiman left the cave one afternoon after a bitter argument with Rafiqa, and that was the last she saw of her husband.

She had not expected him back soon, but when Suleiman didn't return even after three weeks, Rafiqa declared an emergency. She tried to make contact with Suleiman's friends, some of whom had gone out that fateful morning to help the militants. This was no easy job. It involved sending out signals and messages in the most discreet and strange manner, then waiting for days at an end to get even the most insignificant response. Months passed, and Rafiqa turned from a homely, simple woman into a messenger between different stakeholders operating in Kupwara, involving not just members of militant outfits but also security forces. Despite this, she failed to get any concrete piece of information about Suleiman, and soon, her husband, like many other men from within and outside Dardpora, was termed 'missing'. This left her a half-widow, someone who didn't know whether her husband was dead or alive.

In trying to get any news about Suleiman, Rafiqa had many

a time ruffled a few feathers here and there, and had also made many enemies. In order to placate them, she sometimes had to compromise sexually so as to avoid trouble. Before long, she was joined by other women who had similar backgrounds. Soon, Dardpora became known as the infamous village of half-widows whose women were aware of shorter routes in the mountains of Kupwara. They guided both militants as well as security forces through these routes, and in return demanded favours which otherwise would not come their way. Sexual manipulation became a common game played out in the region.

It was early morning by the time Rafiqa finished her story, almost six years since Suleiman had gone 'missing'. I didn't know what to say to her, and sensing my discomfort, she suggested we get out of bed and have some tea. After the morning ritual of tea and breakfast, I expressed a desire to return to Srinagar. I had intimated Hussain the previous day about my plan to return, and he had told me he would wait for me on the outskirts of the village around noon.

Thanking Rafiqa's parents for their hospitality and kindness, I left her home, and saying my goodbyes to everyone I met on the way, Rafiqa and I reached the village border. Sure enough, Hussain was there, and was happy to see me emerge from yet another rendezvous in the mountains. I hugged Rafiqa affectionately; we had previously spoken about how essential it was for the world to know what the women of Dardpora went through in their daily struggle for survival. As I was about to get into Hussain's jeep, I once again urged her to think about the proposed women's conference, and whether she would like to share some details of her life with the other participants.

In my many years of living and working in J&K, Kunan Poshpora, also in Kupwara, is the only place where I have encountered hostility. This is probably the only village where I have no family to call my own, where I cannot simply land up and demand to be indulged.

Kunan Poshpora was raided on 23–24 February 1990 by soldiers from the 4th Rajputana Rifles during a counter-insurgency operation. Under the pretext of search operations, all the men were made to assemble at one place, while the women were mass-raped. Thereafter, the village was nick-named as the 'village of raped women' after the incident got highlighted in the international media. To date, most women from the village remain unmarried because of the stigma attached to this gruesome violation of a woman's body.

The Press Council of India (PCI) conducted an investigation in the village, and concluded that no rape had taken place. The PCI dismissed the allegations of the victims, while their medical reports were withheld. The report said that when investigators went to Kunan Poshpora to find out if the mass rape had actually taken place, they found all the women giggling and laughing. This led them to believe that a heinous crime like rape could not have been committed there, or else the women would not have been laughing![38]

During my first visit, I was not even allowed to go beyond the entrance to the village, let alone talk to anyone. The men were rude and unwelcoming, and almost shooed me away. But my persistence and repeated visits finally resulted in me being able to meet and talk with a few women. It was impossible to tell which ones were physically abused and which ones were scarred simply because they happened to be living in the village. For all of them, the stigma of belonging to the 'village of raped women' was something they had to learn to live with. At first, it seemed highly insensitive to approach people, especially women, for my own interests. How could one expect them to respond to an outsider's questions of 'what happened'! But once my presence in the village was beginning to get accepted, there was nothing else one could talk about.

One woman from Kunan Poshpora told me it was important for them to go about the daily chores of everyday life and maintain the façade of 'normalcy' because everything would just come crashing down and their worlds would completely collapse if they didn't. It made me wonder whether the women were living in denial, or were simply not willing to acknowledge to themselves (more than anyone else) what had happened as they feared a complete breakdown of their lives.

During my repeated visits to Kunan Poshpora, I came to know of Sharifa, a mother of six children who committed suicide along with another raped woman; of seven sisters who were gang-raped and left to fend for themselves; of a nine-month pregnant woman who delivered a child three days after she was gang-raped by eight jawans – both the child's arms were fractured; of Bano, who delivered a five-and-a-half-month-old foetus two weeks after she was raped. Luckily for her, the dismembered child was dead. A J&K Armed Police jawan was tied to a post and forced to watch the gang rape of his 70-year-old grandmother, 45-year-old mother and 18-year-old sister.

It is difficult to explain my state of mind after I had visited the village a few times. I was on the verge of a nervous breakdown, and therefore chose solitude to deal with this horror. I needed to be alone, and I chose to go into hiding in Rasheed sa'ab's houseboat. After a few days, that, too, was uncomfortable, and as usual, I sought Sukanya's company and wisdom. I told her I couldn't deal with what I had experienced in the last few weeks. We had a long discussion about my motive for visiting the village. She gently made me ponder over whether my going there again and again would serve towards my so-called purpose of identifying and then persuading a woman from Kunan Poshpora to join the women's conference. She even chided me for allowing my emotions to get the better of me.

Sukanya put things in perspective. She told me that girls from the village were teased and taunted even now, including by men from their own village. The terror and humiliation faced by the victims was unbelievable. She made me question myself about whether my repeated visits would help them in any way, or would it be yet another reminder of their circumstances. She offered to make me meet someone from the village, and I gladly took up her offer to meet with Zainab.

I set out to meet Zainab at the appointed hour and place that Sukanya had fixed for us. I wasn't expecting to see a petite and immaculately dressed woman who introduced herself as Zainab. She told me she taught a course on 'Gender and Conflict' at the Kashmir University's M.A. programme. Since Sukanya was the common factor between us, I assumed there was no need to build the ground for my reasons for meeting her, and I told her exactly why I was there.

She smiled at me, and said, 'Age-old customs and traditions reaffirm that women's bodies are meant to be used for men's amusement, and they don't have an independent stand or value. In such a case, women become more vulnerable in times of conflict. There are restrictions on women's mobility, ban on contraception, the increased incidences of rape and abductions (as in the case of Dardpora and Kunan Poshpora), and absence of infrastructure to deal with women's reproductive health needs. Needless to say, this only worsens the scenario for women in Kashmir.'

We sat across each other sipping coffee, as we were meeting at one of the few coffee shops in Srinagar: Hotel Broadway's Café Arabica. There was an instant camaraderie between us, and Zainab felt comfortable enough to share her life with me. Born in Kunan Poshpora in a joint family, she was a bright child. After her initial years in the local village school, her father sent her to the city, under the care of his sister, who was married into a family based in the Khanyar area of old Srinagar. Zainab finished her schooling, and was soon enrolled at the graduate studies programme at Kashmir University. Political unrest in Kashmir had already begun around this time, and apart from education, Zainab also received exposure to the world of politics, conflict, diplomacy (or the lack of it) and international affairs.

Whenever she would get a few days off from university, Zainab would go home to Kunan Poshpora and spend time with her family. As luck would have it, she was at her parents' home on the fateful day of the raid by the Rajputana Rifles. She, too, got engulfed in the fire that burnt almost every woman in the village. Thereafter, the term 'difficult circumstances' took on a new meaning for her. She had to fight with her family to go back to university. Once she came back, hardly a day went by that she wasn't reminded about the incident, either by fellow students or by some situation or incident. Still, Zainab continued with her studies, and surprised everyone with her resilience. According to her, she could not have afforded to indulge in self-pity. She needed to get back to 'normal' life, and there was no other route to it except through university.

I did not have the heart to ask Zainab for any more details. The fact that she chose to take life in her stride and deal with it rather than blame fate spoke volumes about her. Her journey from the day of the raid to the day she began teaching 'gender and conflict' would have been anything but normal and an everyday affair for her. She was yet another example of how women were tossed around in this conflict, caught between warring forces.

While militants and security forces have targeted and harassed women in the most brutal ways – Dardpora and Kunan Poshpora being just two examples out of the hundreds of such cases – the governments – state as well as Central – have either ignored women in their rehabilitation schemes and/or relief packages, or done minuscule work towards re-settling their lives. In such a scenario, the onus is on civil society organizations working in Kashmir to strongly take up the cause of women.

In Kunan Poshpora, apart from the atrocities on women, none of the stakeholders have questioned medical facilities or the lack of same, especially for women. Kashmir has many government hospitals and sponsored healthcare clinics, but the more-than-two-decades-long conflict has resulted in the exodus of qualified medical professionals. Government medical facilities remain short-staffed and inadequate for meeting even the basic health needs of people. The doctors who remain in Kashmir (most go away to other Indian cities or abroad) prefer to be based in the cities, leading to a complete collapse of the healthcare system in the villages. And in a society where women's needs are secondary to men's in almost everything, their healthcare needs are not even an issue!

After my visits to Dardpora and Kunan Poshpora and having dealt with the emotional aspect of it, I couldn't help but wonder how these two events in the lives of two communities from two different villages would have affected the collective psyche of the community. Rafiqa's story was of course personal; yet, it was the story of every other woman in Kashmir who had lost her man – be it her father, brother, uncle, husband or son – to the political upheaval. What had happened in Kunan Poshpora was beyond words. The incidents were gory, violent and horrific. People's identities, especially the women's, dominated everything else. In an attempt to 'settle scores' and to offend the 'other', certain elements – whether they were security forces or militants – apart from pillaging and killing had thought it appropriate to violate the bodies of women.

When I spoke to the people about these incidents – both victims and witnesses – there were odd silences, where people were obviously 'editing' as they spoke: revealing only what was fit for consumption. Obviously, this 'selective memory' was a technique and a powerful tool to overcome trauma. The human heart chose to remember and narrate only that which it could deal with; what it couldn't deal with was purposely erased from personal as well as public memory.

Over the course of my work in Kashmir, I had experienced other people's trauma. To me, counselling and healing was not just understanding others' pain and reducing their stress; it was also a matter of being non-judgmental about the events in their lives. As a counsellor, I may have derived satisfaction from sharing someone's pain, but I was equally aware and conscious of the fact that it was a matter of great honour for people to consider me empathetic enough to share their secrets. I may not have been able to provide solutions to all their problems, but I certainly cared. It was a relationship of mutual concern and acceptance.

On my part, I found comfort and solace within the land of Kashmir. It was sheer therapy as the waters of the Dal and Nagin lakes rocked my shikara. It was therapeutic to indulge myself at Beauty Art Palace, on Lambert Lane, next to the Residency Road market, from where I would buy the most intricately designed silver earrings. The owner knew my choice, and he would always keep aside a few pieces of jewellery whenever he got a delivery of fresh stock. This, to me, is Kashmiriyat, too!

# Humsaya & Boonye

*Don't think I did all this to get famous.*
*I never cared for the good things of life.*
*I always ate sensibly. I knew hunger well,*
*and sorrow, and God.*[39]

For some reason, I woke up one day to the thoughts of Asiya Andrabi, president of the Dukhtaran-e-Millat (DeM), or Daughters of the Faith. I had met Asiya a few times, and to me, she was very much the hospitable Kashmiri woman-next-door, very unlike the personification of the firebrand woman separatist 'leader'. When in public, her eyes are the only visible parts of her body, the rest securely covered by the burqa. Even her hands are covered with gloves. I couldn't help comparing Asiya's DeM with that of the NC's 1947 women's militia.

Asiya had made headlines for her group members throwing acid on the faces of women who refused to wear the burqa, and for her protests and statements against those involved in the sex scandal which rocked the Kashmir valley in 2005. As the head of the only organization of women separatists in Kashmir, also interpreted by many as the only women's militant group operating for over twenty-five years now, she told me once, 'I don't believe in equality of the sexes. Rather, it is equity for women that I push for.'

I had read some of Asiya's press interviews before I first met her in 2005. She had mentioned in detail the torture and trauma she had undergone whilst she had been in jail a few times since the year 2000. Her outfit DeM had been banned since 1990, and the Indian government had accused her of various anti-national activities, including staging anti-India rallies by the DeM activists and protesting against the atrocities committed by Indian security forces in Kashmir. As we sat in her home, talking and playing with her nieces and nephews, it was difficult for me to understand the change of heart she must have gone through to leave her studies (she was a bright student, according to reports), and a very fashion-conscious lifestyle to marry a mujahid and lead the kind of 'separatist' life that she does.

After the DeM was formed in 1981, the 'women activists' of the organization came on the streets in 1987 to fight for reservation of seats for women in public transportation, took action against families that demanded dowry, and arranged marriages for girls from economically backward families. Asiya said, 'Since my brothers were already part of separatist politics, my initiation into the anti-India sentiment happened while

I was still in school. I was used to police raids much before I jumped full-time into the freedom movement. I was enamoured by the heroic deeds of the mujahids and yearned to join the jihad. For me, jihad is not just a means to an end; it is a lifelong mission. Allah says in the Quran that jihad is the only way to uproot evil from this world... And for me, Osama bin Laden symbolizes jihad. He has the courage to challenge the world's superpower, America. As much as I hate George Bush for being the oppressor that he is, I respect and admire bin Laden for his bravery. In fact, I want my sons to follow in his footsteps and serve Islam and Allah the way bin Laden has.'

Asiya and her supporters did enjoy the limelight while it lasted, and basked in its glory. While women taking to the streets were not uncommon in Kashmir, what was unusual was the extremities and theatrics of the DeM. However, Asiya's philosophy found very few takers. Over time, Asiya and the DeM have faded away from the Kashmir conflict, and from public memory, especially in Kashmir.

What Asiya chose to do through aggression and hostility, Jehanara Maqbool chose to do with a graceful display of the common man's antagonism. Asiya's ways demonstrated anger in a violent way; Jehanara displayed unacceptance through refined resentment. Other than Lalla, if there is another Kashmiri woman who fits the description in the *vakh* preceding this chapter, it is Jehanara. She has been synonymous with the struggle of thousands of Kashmiri women and men to locate their missing sons, brothers, husbands and fathers. Before I met her, I had assumed her to be a woman with an air of self-importance and a no-nonsense attitude. I couldn't have been more wrong. She was extremely friendly and unassuming, and spoke passionately about the gross injustice meted out by security forces as she cooked and fed me. It was then that I realised she was my houseboat owner Rasheed sa'ab's older sister.

I had heard her speak many a times about the disappearance of her younger son, Javed, as about the sons of other parents. She had been interviewed by many from the national and international media and civil society organizations over the years, and had narrated her story as patiently to one as to the other, never sounding bitter or disappointed. What she had never told anybody was her own personal story: one of being harassed by her husband and in-laws, and being thrown out of the house. She had no choice but to take refuge in her brother's house who not only looked after her but also looked up to her as someone who could deal with the most difficult of circumstances.

In a complete contrast to Asiya Andrabi, Jehanara had truly captured the essence of UNSCR 1325, without even knowing what it is and what its implication could be. The resolution, passed on 31 October 2000, is the first resolution ever passed by the UN that specifically addresses the impact of war on women and women's contributions to conflict resolution and sustainable peace.

An ordinary Kashmiri girl who quietly turned into an ordinary Kashmiri woman once she was married to Ghulam

Maqbool, Jehanara moved into the house he shared with his parents, his older brother and his family and two younger siblings, both of whom were unmarried. Jehanara bore Maqbool two sons – Javed and Karim. Life seemed normal even amidst the turmoil of the conflict, until one ordinary February day. The family woke up to a smoky, misty dawn for the *fajr* (early morning) prayers. Though the worst of the winter was over, and it wasn't snowing any more, the chill of the season was still palpable. But unlike the *chill-e-kalaan*, the forty-day period of extreme cold, the day would gradually be filled with sunshine. As numerous cups of *noon chai*, the famous salty tea of Kashmir, were passed around and as family members assembled in the kitchen one after the other, Javed's absence was felt.

By nine, when Javed had still not shown up, Ghulam Maqbool went upstairs to his room to check. But his son was not there. After searching the whole house and the neighbourhood, Maqbool pressed the panic button. It was usual for Javed to hang out with his friends until late in the night, and quietly slip into the house without disturbing anybody. This habit, though not appreciated or encouraged by the elders, was an everyday feature. Maqbool immediately went to Javed's closest friend, Rafiq. He didn't have to go any further. Rafiq narrated the incidents of the previous night, when the friends were hanging out as usual. A Maruti Gypsy emerged out of nowhere, and the police took Javed away without any explanation. The only apology of a reason they offered was that his name had come up in a bomb blast incident which had happened in Lal Chowk the previous week, and so they had taken him away for questioning. When the friends tried to intervene, they were bashed up, explaining the swollen eye and cuts on Rafiq's hands and arms. Kashmir had seen too many such 'disappearances' of young and old men alike to either question them or to not know what had conspired. Still, the father left no stone unturned to find his missing son, but his efforts were futile.

Eventually, Javed's disappearance was blamed on Jehanara and her mode of upbringing. Though the reasoning was neither obvious nor justified, she quietly took all the blame. The atmosphere at home turned hostile, and lines of communication, especially between Jehanara and Maqbool, snapped. She kept up the effort, nevertheless, and the hope to find Javed. She got in touch with other families who had gone through a similar set of circumstances, and sadly, there were many of them in Kashmir.

Without any formal platform and/or family support, Jehanara found her own personal Azaadi by mobilizing and bringing together people and families who had lost their near and dear ones to the conflict. She chose to overcome her personal tragedy and give an empathetic ear to other such mothers, wives, sisters and daughters. She created her own platform – 'Finding the Missing' (FM) – to tell the government that such atrocities and human rights violations were unacceptable. FM became synonymous with the people's struggle against the tyranny of the government and its forces, and a collective effort to seek information about the whereabouts of the thousands of missing people.

FM was a people's movement in its own right: while some groups of women went from one police station to the next demanding to know where their relatives were, others did the rounds of interrogation centres. Yet others wandered around camps and hospitals looking for any signs and traces that could lead them to their 'missing' men. Once a month, the group would assemble at a public park and stage a silent protest against the government. However, the number of disappearances continued to increase, leading to more unrest. After visiting police stations for several months at an end, a court case was finally registered towards Jehanara's plea to trace her missing son, as it was for a few others. However, the court did little other than issue an order for inquiry into the matter. Meanwhile, the Army offered her a few lakh rupees and some additional 'perks' if Jehanara chose to withdraw her case. Naturally, she refused to sell her son and his memories.

This people's uprising was completely non-violent. It involved not just running from pillar to post in the hope of finding a link towards the missing, but also led to ignoring home and family for justice. Such a situation happened to Jehanara as well. In the years that she spent running from police stations and hospitals to courts and from interrogation centres to jails, her old parents-in-law died a sad death. Maqbool's older brother, Rauf, chose to move out with his wife and their two children. The younger brother, Salim, left for Delhi in pursuit of higher studies and some kind of a future, and the sister, Salima, got married to a local guy. Her younger son, Karim, had already been moved out of the valley. Distant relatives in Dehradun had given the boy a refuge in their home and hearts, and the boy grew up feeling loved but uprooted.

Meanwhile, Jehanara led two different lives. Her days were occupied with being the pillar of support that she had become for all those who were realizing how malicious the word 'missing' could be. Her nights, however, were restless and sleepless. When she did occasionally drift into sleep, it was the same, recurrent dream each night:

> 'A grey, cloudy day; a huge maidan; thousands of men, young and old, trying to brave the chill with their respective *pherans*; emotions running high; the crowd swelling up with every minute... The day is 13 July, Martyr's Day, marked since 1931 as the day twenty-one peaceful demonstrators were gunned down under the Dogra leadership. At a peaceful demonstration in observance of Martyr's Day, without any provocation, the security forces start to fire indiscriminately. Several people are killed, and hundreds of others seriously wounded. Since the city is shut down anyway, there is not much help forthcoming. What follows is a deafening silence.'

It was at this point that Jehanara always woke up, profusely shaken up, her heart almost at a standstill.

For some bizzare reason, Jehanara's dream brought to my mind an incident that a friend of mine told me about. Bashir was in his teens when his father, Ghulam Rasool Shah, launched a daily newspaper in 1992 at the peak of the Kashmiri insurgency. Over the years, it had become one of the most respected Urdu newspapers in the region. 'Those were tough times,' Bashir recalled. 'My father was kidnapped for a week by the *ikhwanis* (surrendered militants), as they wanted more coverage of their activities. Kukka Parrey, their leader, accused us of not publishing news about them. On the other side were the militants, who warned us against publishing anything about the *ikhwanis*. The Army was also after us. But not for one day did the newspaper close down.' The one-week kidnapping finally ended with Shah promising to publish more news about the *ikhwanis*, and with Parrey giving him two identical photographs of himself surrounded by his gunmen and demanding both pictures be published on page one of the newspaper.

During the captivity, however, Bashir and his family members had approached a senior hard-line separatist for help. 'He told us that 50–60,000 people had died in Kashmir, and nothing was wrong if my father's name was added to the list,' Bashir said. Eventually, Shah published the two photographs and the family waited with baited breath for any retaliation. 'Thank God nothing happened,' Bashir told me.

For those who decided to leave behind arms and join the mainstream – the *ikhwanis* – it has been a regretful decision. With a meagre insurance and promises of a job that were almost never fulfilled, life was a constant routine of reporting to the local police station every week, spending days in a lock-up before a public event to avoid any suspected 'mischief', and torture in the event of a violent incident.

When I met with some of these men and their families, it seemed more often than not that the men had just gone along with the flow of the freedom movement and then suddenly decided one day that it wasn't their thing, not necessarily wanting to drift away from the affairs of either the state or Kashmir politics. They simply found themselves wound up in a whirlpool of events that were beyond their control. As far as their women were concerned, they didn't know what had hit them. They were not sure what to make of their men – whether to be proud of them or to lament the fact that they didn't know what they wanted to do: either with themselves or with their families.

At Bashir's wedding, as Shah sahib and I sat recounting this incident, he told me, '*Kya karenge, yeh sab toh chalta hai yahan* (What to do, all this goes on here)', and nudged the tray of dry fruits towards me. As we chatted, Shah sahib and I, sitting on the plush Kashmiri carpet, Bashir's phone rang. He did not react but gave the phone to his father and explained, 'The maulvi is now conducting the marriage ceremony at my bride's house. Someone has called so that we can listen in.' After a few minutes, Bashir's father hugged him. His mother and sister, too, came and hugged him. He was now a married man: the bride had said 'yes'! The house burst into celebrations; the singing reached a crescendo: 'Go and get your bride, she is waiting for you; they will put a gold crown on your head, go soon, she is waiting for you ...'

The following evening, as we left as part of the *baaraat* to bring the bride home, we came across the first security camp just five minutes away from Bashir's house. There were no street lights and at nine in the night, most people had gone to sleep. Like a well-rehearsed ritual, all the cars slowed down before the camp, switched off the headlights and switched on the cabin lights for the security men to see who was inside. They let us pass without any checks and the gun-toting soldiers even smiled and waved at us as the caravan of cars went by – a rarity. My only thought was, how do I reconcile this with the 'Two killed, twelve wounded in Kashmir gunbattle' headline that kept screaming from the newspapers?

Meanwhile, something dreadful had happened in Ladakh. Leh and some parts of Kargil were hit by a cloudburst and subsequent floods in the early morning hours of an August day in 2010. The cloudburst led to so much rain that most of the city of Leh and its adjoining villages got washed away in half-an-hour, and many villages towards Kargil also suffered considerable damage. The local people, the administration and everyone else were completely unprepared for such a calamity.

When I had first visited Ladakh the previous year, I went by road from Leh to Kargil and then from Kargil to Srinagar – a journey unlike any other. At one point, on the way from Leh to village Nemo, the Indus meets with the Zanskar, and nothing is more striking than the sight of the muddy brown waters of the former merging with the sparkling deep blue waters of the latter. The meeting point is duly called Sangam, and the two rivers, after they have merged, continue to flow as the Indus till Batalik, and then move into Pakistan.

The enormous mountains, which had initially seemed very inhospitable, changed many shades and colours and became friendlier as we got used to each other. The Ladakhi landscape was a complete contrast to that of the valley. Ladakh surprised me with hard, rigid and barren landscapes that seemed almost unwelcoming in their appearance, but had an unmatched beauty about them. The mountains stood proud and majestic. Despite the beauty, many BRO signposts that said something akin to 'you are being watched by the enemy' were reminders that one was very close to the border; that there was danger lurking at every corner. I briefly stopped over at Khalsti for a quick snack as it was the last point one could get any food until Kargil. I was told very gently, but in no uncertain terms, that it was not advisable to stop anywhere for very long.

The Nubra valley in Ladakh is a different world altogether, housing the peculiarities of two distinct mountain ranges – the Himalayas and the Karakoram. If God intended to hide this valley, to keep it isolated and therefore protected, He did a great job. A desert, complete with sand dunes and two-humped camels, magnificent rivers (Nubra and Shyok) with their beaches, forests and mountains – lush greenery as well as barrenness – all in the same landscape. I decided to stay overnight in village Turtuk, in the valley. Pakistan wasn't far away; just around the corner, across the mountain that sat rigidly in front of me. Everything was in perfect harmony.

Travelling from village Shey (ahead of Leh) to Nubra, I had to cross Khardung-la, the highest motorable road in the world. In a land where black-top roads are a novelty, I was surprised to observe that the road from Hunder onwards was near-perfect. Considering this was a border area, and anything could happen any time, I guessed the authorities did not want to take a chance.

The 'border' scenario was completed by a helipad and many such reminders of the presence of the Army.

I was told to visit Nemo, since it was known for its woman *panch* (head) who contested the Panchayati Raj elections in 2001 and got elected to the village council. Tashi Yangskit was the first and only female voice in the first Panchayati Raj elections held in the state. Tashi welcomed me into her home like it was the most natural thing to do. I brought up the subject of the elections and her subsequent selection to the village council. She seemed to think it was nothing extraordinary. As part of the council, she tried to highlight the tough life Ladakhi women lead. But local politics within the council and the village ensured her voice didn't reach very far, and very soon, Tashi's voice was not taken very seriously.

In Leh, I also met Helena Norberg-Hodge, who had spent many years in Ladakh trying to change the consciousness of the people by bringing about slow and subtle changes in their lifestyle, but taking immense care that the culture and sensibilities of its people were preserved. In her book *Ancient Futures*[40], she expresses her 'deep appreciation for the traditional Ladakhi way of life, as well as some concern for its future', in the words of the Dalai Lama. When I brought up the subject of Ladakhi women, Norberg-Hodge said she was 'struck by their wide, uninhibited smiles. Despite the extremely tough and physically laborious lifestyles they led, they were open and [not] self-conscious, and exhibited great self-confidence, strength of character, and dignity.'

After Nemo, I went up to Darchiks, the last village in the Batalik sector, which is under Army surveillance due to its proximity to the LoC. I had to seek permission from the Biama Brigade to go up to Darchiks, one of the few places supposedly inhabited by the last few surviving Aryans (Aryans are considered to be the semi-nomadic tribe which wandered into India from Central Europe around 1500 BCE). The Army had set up a women's empowerment centre here where women were taught tailoring – something I have grudged for years. Any civil society initiative for women ends up in tailoring/embroidery schools, as if women can't do anything else. However, I also do realize that this is something which comes naturally to women; something that does not need too much 'exposure'!

The high point of this journey was a visit to the Drass War Memorial. Drass and Kargil became household names after the infamous summer of 1999. National Highway 1D passes through Drass, connecting Srinagar and Leh. The town also happens to be the coldest inhabited place in India. Situated between Tiger Hill, Tololing and Three Pimples – the three ranges captured by the Pakistani Army in early 1999 during the Kargil war – the memorial was awe-inspiring, to say the least. In the soldiers' accounts accompanying the many photographs at the memorial, there is one in particular that struck me: the climate was so harsh even during the summer that 'eggs become tennis balls, and orange juice has to be boiled'. I made a mental note of coming back to spend more time there.

As I was leaving, I thanked the soldier on duty who had very patiently and kindly answered all my questions, and shown me around. Overwhelmed with emotion, I told him that it was because of him and innumerable other jawans like him that people like me were walking 'free'. He returned the compliment by saying civilians were equally important. He went on further to say that thousands of people worked hard day and night to prepare food and warm clothing, and arranged to carry weaponry etc. uphill so that the soldiers could fight, and eventually win the war. I couldn't remember a more humbling moment!

The visit to the memorial made me dwell on the futility of war – certainly nothing original, but something very personal. Fifteen years since Kargil, have India and Pakistan moved forward on any front? Leave alone the larger Indo-Pak issues, have we moved any further on the cross-border/intra-Kashmir initiatives?

The contrast between the women from Kargil and Leh was quite striking. Of course the basic difference in their cultures was that Leh is a Buddhist-dominated land whereas Kargil is a Muslim-dominated area. Whilst women in Leh spoke to me openly, outdoors, and with no inhibitions whatsoever, the women in Kargil chose to speak to me from behind walls, within the confines of their homes and most of them did not even raise their *niqab*! They spoke in hushed tones, and their primary concern was to educate their girls and work out some way of 'family planning'. Despite this, I met Shah Bano here, who, against all the odds, had the courage to raise her voice against atrocities on Muslim women in Kargil. She had even tried to contest a seat from a political party, and was punished for daring to challenge a male-dominated society. She and her family received death threats, and after a while it was almost impossible for her to step out of her house.

On this second trip to Ladakh, which was about ten days after the cloudburst, I was visiting as part of a team that was to assess the damage and reconstruct houses for the families which had lost their homes to the flood. At the same time, I wanted to meet with the local women to get a flavour of their daily lives. There were no fixed numbers on how many people had died and how many were missing. Leh was the hub of 'disaster tourism' at this point, attracting not just national NGOs and charity organizations but also foreign groups offering support. According to early media reports, Leh and the adjoining villages of Choglamsar and Nemo were the worst affected by the floods.[41] I did visit Nemo again to contact Tashi, but I couldn't meet her in the confusion of the disaster. I didn't have the courage to ask the villagers whether she was dead or alive. I let her be one of the many anonymous people who were there (or not there) amidst the uncertainty of the surroundings. It seemed selfish to meet people, especially women, with the women's workshop as the underlying motive. I decided to set up base in Leh city, visit some villages, and not worry too much about finding that one woman from Ladakh who would represent her land at my forthcoming conference.

Travelling to remote and inaccessible villages was not easy as one had to negotiate hostile topography amongst the mountains where black-top roads are difficult to find. On many occasions, I managed to visit only one village in the entire day because the terrain was such, or the village was several hundred kilometres from Leh, or there was a jam owing to the BRO's efforts to clear up debris from the mountains, or all of these reasons. During one such jam, we overheard a group of Army jawans interact with a group of jawans from the Punjab Police, who were discussing everything, from the sudden orders to go to Leh to the changing weather. They even talked of militancy in Punjab and compared it to that in Kashmir. Their jolly mood helped to lighten the heaviness of the jam.

The villages I went to were full of apricot and apple trees and seabuckthorn shrubs, all laden with so much fruit that the trees were bending with the weight. Thankfully they had not been washed away in the flood. Children played in the mud as women went about their daily chores, while the men were busy in the fields. It all seemed very normal, but once I entered the interiors of the village, it was evident that the place had witnessed something not-so-natural: roads and bridges had been washed away; miles of land had been buried under debris; houses and shops had been destroyed beyond recognition; people were rendered homeless, and the hungry and the abandoned had to face a severe winter.

After interacting with the locals, I gathered that while the loss of life and property was lamented upon, the people were also very upset that several Buddhist gompas, monasteries and prayer wheels had also suffered a lot of damage in the floods. While much land and property was damaged and lost, there were many buildings that were saved from the floods, despite the adjoining construction being lost to the waters. Many opined that the devastation in Leh was centred around what may have been a waterway decades or even centuries ago. These areas, where there probably were gushing streams or other water bodies, were slowly taken over by 'civilization' over the years, and people used the land for constructing homes and hearths. It was these buildings that had been constructed on a dried riverbed from the past that got destroyed – one of nature's many ways of re-claiming that which humans had taken away.

One of the many explanations for the flash floods was that enthusiastic environmentalists had tried to make Ladakh 'green'. Ladakh is a cold desert, much along the lines of the Tundra, and is not meant to have 'greenery'. The reasoning is that all the trees that have been planted over the decades have caused precipitation, and this precipitation, accumulated over time, is what resulted in the calamity. Even the apricot and apple trees which Ladakh is renowned for are not natural to this land; rather, the trees are native to the adjoining areas of Himachal and Kashmir.

One area that is particularly known for its apricots or *chuli*, as it is known locally, is Hanu. The main village here is called Dah Hanu; the lower reaches are known as Hanu Yogma, and the parts of the village based in the higher ranges of the mountains are called Hanu Gongma. It is here that the word 'exotic' can be fully applied, with its blue-eyed women with extraordinary embellishments in their knee-length braids; men with perfect physiques; unusual and exquisite contours in the land; and in the generosity and abundance of nature.

When I had visited Ladakh the previous year, I had managed to drive up to a place called Ganasok, supposedly a 'restricted area' where only the Army is allowed movement. I had wanted to visit Dah Hanu, and having lost my way, I ended up driving into this 'highly protected area' that had no signage to tell me it was a restricted area. I was not even stopped at the two check posts on my way up, apparently because I was driving a Maruti Gypsy, the official car in the mountains. When I was finally intercepted at Ganasok, I was told I had managed to do something no civilian had done in the past twelve years – no mean achievement! The high security here is because of its close proximity to the Pakistan border; civilian entry is not permitted and only special guests of the Army are allowed access to the region.

It was to Dah Hanu that I was making my way yet again when I was stopped by a woman in her late sixties. She was carrying a huge basket of apricots on her back, and she wanted a lift to Hanu Gongma, where she lived. I opened the door of my jeep to accommodate her and her basket, along with the several layers of her traditional Ladakhi outfit, her tiny shells and hair accessories, her numerous rings and bangles and the belt fastened around her waist, complete with a set of several bells – all of which made her seem like straight out of *Alice in Wonderland*! The gypsy woman, as I mentally tagged her, had a generous smile which set her face in several layers of wrinkles. As soon as she settled herself, she unwound her prayer beads from around her wrist, and started turning them. As a token of thanks, she filled her palms with a generous number of apricots and deposited them in my lap, gesturing at me to eat them. I sampled them and the pleasure evident on my face made my gypsy woman smile. Just as I was thinking that smiles would be our only method of communication, she asked me my name and where I was coming from, in Hindi. We soon struck up a conversation, and the half-hour drive up to Hanu Gongma was very informative and entertaining.

My gypsy woman, Sonam Lobzang, invited me to her house. I accepted her invitation gratefully, as my bones were feeling rattled after the seven-hour drive from Leh to Dah Hanu. She asked for the jeep to be stopped by a huge prayer wheel, and as we got off the vehicle, I asked her where her home was. I could see no human dwelling in the vast expanse of the mountain in front of us, its monotony broken only by saffron fields in full bloom, their yellow flowers making it a more-than-idyllic setting for a romantic rendezvous. Sonam smiled her incredible smile and told me it was a ten-minute walk down the mountain where we stood. Of course, my city-bred sensibilities did realize that a ten-minute walk for her meant a half-an-hour struggle for me. What I didn't realize, however, was that we had to climb down a steep slope where I slipped several times, and the drama would be complete with us crossing a gushing, gurgling stream over a narrow wooden bridge that seemed ready to collapse any minute!

We finally reached Sonam's house, which was bordered by the stream on one side and saffron fields on the other. Her cattle and three dogs looked at me suspiciously as we entered her kitchen. She talked to her animals in the most loving manner, introduced us to each other, and as if on cue, the dogs came and settled themselves all around me. After a refreshing cup of tea and an offer to stay with her for as long as I liked, Sonam asked me if I would like to walk around the village with her; I was more than eager and happy to do so. She carried her huge apricot basket with her, and we set off. Each of the houses in the village was quite a distance from the other, and it was a pleasant experience as we negotiated our way – Sonam with the precision and agility of a mountain goat, and me floundering behind her, trying miserably to keep pace.

As we visited different homes, it was clear that the flood had turned people's lives upside-down, but there was no negativity in their demeanour. They undertook the task of re-building their lives with the utmost simplicity and with so much conviction as if it were the most natural thing to do. Sonam offered her support, encouragement and handfuls of *chuli* to everyone she met, never forgetting to introduce me to each and every one. As people greeted us, I could sense the awe in the way they met Sonam. When we finished meeting about eight to ten families, she suggested we go back and meet the others in the coming days. It was on the way back that I got an opportunity to ask her about her life.

A mother of three daughters and two sons, Sonam had two husbands, one of whom had died many years ago, and the second was with the Army, posted in Himachal. It was common for the women in Ladakh, especially in rural Ladakh, to have several husbands – in most cases, brothers sharing one wife – because it meant that the land and/or property would remain undivided. It was also common to have other lovers, particularly in the case of women like Sonam, who didn't have any husband living with her. Sex was not a big deal, and Ladakhis seemed very liberal in their approach towards relationships between men and women.

Sonam had pretty much been her own person, even as a child.

Whilst she was unmarried, she had to take on the responsibility of her family after her mother died. She never went to school, instead taking care of her siblings, who were children then, and maintaining the house. Married at the age of fourteen to two brothers, Sonam did not have an easy life. After both her husbands went away, she was single-handedly responsible for her and her children's lives.

By now, we had reached Sonam's home, and she told me we would talk more in the evening as she needed to finish off some chores and prepare the evening meal. The air was nippy, and the warmth of Sonam's kitchen was a very welcome relief from the chill outside. All her children were married, and lived in and around Hanu Gongma. We were joined by her younger son and his wife, who helped Sonam as she served everyone *chang*, the local liquor. As her son prepared rice and vegetables, we were joined by an older man. Nobody introduced me to him, but it was understood that he was the man of the house – Sonam's companion. I was made to feel completely 'at home', and soon everyone was talking to everyone, sharing small details of how the day had been for all of us.

After the meal, we sat around the fire, with Sonam insisting on everyone having generous helpings of almonds to keep warm. When I asked her about the four-year-old girl and the toddler, probably ten months old, who were in the house at all times, she said they were her oldest daughter's children. Her daughter had died a few months ago, and she did not trust her in-laws to bring them up with love and care. She had therefore fought with them bitterly, and even paid them money to take on the responsibility.

I woke up quite early the next morning, as my watch indicated, but it was obviously late enough for the whole household to be going about their chores, including the cattle, who made a ruckus demanding everyone's attention, especially Sonam's. I was offered smiles and hot tea, and settled into a comfortable corner of the kitchen. Everything seemed so different and extraordinary: there was no rush; there were no deadlines whatsoever; time seemed to be inconsequential; and the day's routine had a rhythm of its own.

After breakfast, which consisted of a home-made preparation of flour and white butter, and endless cups of yak's milk tea, Sonam and I left to meet some more families affected by the flood. It was an opportune moment to talk to her about my proposed women's workshop, and I extended an invitation to her, expressing a strong desire for her to join us. She did not give me a definite answer, but her look said: You have lived with me in my home; therefore, you are my very own. I will do whatever makes you happy!

# Yogini

*I, Lalla, wore myself down searching for Him*
*and found a strength after my strength had died.*
*I came to His threshold but found the door bolted.*
*I unlocked that door with my eyes and looked at Him.*[42]

My first informal meeting towards the proposed women's workshop was with Jehanara, Rafiqa and Ananya: Jehanara, who began with her personal struggle, got engulfed by the larger struggle of 'missing men' in Kashmir, and somewhere merged the two; Rafiqa, who wasn't sure whether she had a husband or not, and whether she could lay any claims to her husband's family; and Ananya, who had grown up in unfriendly circumstances, and was defining her space through her writings.

Ananya, with whom my acquaintance was relatively new, was not sure of how to interpret my moves – whether to categorize me as someone who came to Kashmir for her work and made the most of Kashmiris, or whether to believe in what seemed like genuine reasons to connect with various stakeholders in Kashmir. Jehanara, of course, had taken on the responsibility to mother me, as she did for everyone else. My association with Rasheed sa'ab and her almost made me a member of their family, which was both good and bad, for varied reasons. Rafiqa had known me for several years. Since the time she and I had travelled to her village Dardpora, we had broken new ground in terms of familiarity, and Rafiqa was no longer shy of talking to me.

When I reached the venue of our meeting, which was in the beautiful expanse of the Nishat Bagh in Srinagar, Rafiqa was already there, lost in her own thoughts, or perhaps mesmerized by what she saw around her. Located on the banks of the Dal Lake, with the Zabarwan hills forming a splendid background, the Nishat Bagh gardens command a magnificent view of the Pir Panjal mountain range. Built by Empress Noor Jehan's father, Asif Khan, in 1633 CE, the Bagh was initially laid out as a broad cascade of twelve terraces representing the twelve zodiac signs. However, what remain today are only nine terraces; three of them have given way to the vagaries of time and nature.

I chose Nishat Bagh, lined with chinar and cypress trees, as our meeting point as I thought its natural beauty would aid us in our efforts to connect. Ananya and Jehanara came almost one after the other, and after the initial introductions, we sat under a chinar tree, not sure where to begin. Jehanara promptly produced a flask of cinnamon-flavoured *kahwa* and *bakerkhani,* one of the local Kashmiri breads baked fresh every morning at almost every corner in the valley. This eased the tension a bit, and we slowly settled down to a casual chit-chat about the goings-on. Jehanara mentioned that yet another young man had gone 'missing' in her neighbourhood the previous week. She was convinced the boy was a harmless soul, but the police had come on their usual rounds, found the boy and picked him up for questioning. When he did not return home even after twenty-four hours, the boy's parents raised an alarm and went looking for him. Of course the local police station denied they had picked up the boy. The parents had then come to Jehanara. She was trying to follow-up on the boy's disappearance at her own level, through her platform 'Finding the Missing'. She remarked, 'Many Muslim men go missing,' to which Ananya reacted very strongly.

Ananya had grown up seeing men being brutalized and manhandled. The migrant camps of Jammu were full of men who were living witnesses to the injustice of the exodus. Jehanara's casual comment about Muslim men going missing triggered a chain reaction that came out as a detailed description of life in a migrant camp: the one-room set-ups that served as living room, bedroom and kitchen, all in one; the fact that four families had to share one washroom; the non-existent water supply, drainage and sewage systems, electricity connections...

Jehanara, whose own son had gone missing in the conflict, had chosen to rise above her personal tragedy and support other families who couldn't trace their missing men. Though she did not take Ananya's verbal outburst personally, she did seem hurt by her insensitivity towards the larger issue of human suffering.

Meanwhile, Rafiqa, who neither had Ananya's fiery temper or exposure to the outside world nor the maturity and sensitivity of Jehanara, felt out of place in the whole situation. At the same time, she did not want to be left out. We reached a point of uncomfortable silence that was threatening to break all channels of communication. Seeing this as an opportunity, Rafiqa spoke for the first time. She said she could understand where Ananya and Jehanara were coming from and that she could empathize with them on the issue of their men. Her own husband had gone 'missing', and she was a 'half-widow', ridiculous in every sense of the word. She said there was no point in looking at the issue from either a Hindu or Muslim perspective. The question was how to strengthen women like them to enable them to go through their own personal tragedies.

Though Jehanara and Ananya were momentarily taken aback by the profundity of Rafiqa's thought, the recent clash of words and thoughts did not allow them to ponder over it for too long. Again, the silence was too loud. I was unable to lighten up the heaviness of the situation and therefore suggested we meet again after a few days. The sky had begun to turn pink and the birds began to return to their nests as the day came to an end. The four of us bade embarrassed and muffled goodbyes to each other and said we would be in touch and meet up soon.

This incident reminded me of an earlier visit to Doda district, except that had been a complete contrast to what had happened just now. Doda is about eight to ten hours away from Jammu. The local bus I was travelling on had stopped a couple of times for tea and lunch, and I was quite amused at the observation that nothing united Hindus and Muslims better than Kishore Kumar's songs. Buses and taxis, shops and even some humble eating joints in that part of the Chenab valley played Kishore da, and were joined in by enthusiastic locals.

Later, as I was meeting with people in some of the villages of Doda, the chief priest of the village mosque in Ghat told me, 'Hindus in Doda have a lot of knowledge about Islam, and Muslims in Doda are aware of Hinduism's teachings. Issues like untouchability, which are common elsewhere, are not present in Doda. People here have not received too much exposure, Western concepts have yet to reach us and therefore life is simple and uncomplicated. The problem begins when people with vested interests and political agendas use this simplicity to their advantage and speak ill about one community to another. Until now, Doda was far removed from such issues, but one can sense some tension in the air after the Kulhand massacre.'

In May 2006, nearly two dozen Hindus had been killed in Kulhand village of Doda, disrupting the otherwise peaceful existence of the two major communities.[43] After the incident, communal harmony had prevailed under the constant gaze of the gun – both of the militants and security forces. While militants had lurked in the apple orchards and inaccessible forests, the security forces had guarded each hill-top.

Meanwhile, I had reached my guestroom in Rasheed sa'ab's houseboat after the women's meeting, and began to ponder over my inability and inadequacy as a coordinator. The meeting had left me tense and unsure of myself. I was questioning my ability to deal with the enormity of the task I was hoping to undertake. I needed to distract myself to maintain my sanity. I called Sukanya's residence to check if she was free to meet up.

Zooni's urgent 'hello' told me something was out of place. In a broken voice, she told me Sukanya had moved on to the next world earlier that morning. I was left numb; this information took some time to sink in and register. There was no coherence to the thoughts and emotions that crossed my mind thereafter. How could Sukanya Parashar cease to exist, simply because her heart decided to stop beating? She had helped me shape the conference, but more than the loss of a principal participant, it was the loss of a mentor and guide, a friend who had never failed to support me as much with her thoughts and ideas as with her physical presence. It was through the many conversations we had had that I had lived and experienced a Kashmir free of guns and militants, a place that could truly be called paradise on earth. We had spoken of a Kashmir where a Hindu Pandit family had, for generations, been caretakers of a Muslim shrine; where the people of Kashmir were simply Kashmiris and not Pandits and Muslims. There was a special word for neighbours and friends – *humsaaya*, or 'my very own'. Sukanya's ideal Kashmir was now a ground for negotiations between India and Pakistan. Instead of Sufiana *kalaams* and Lal Ded's poetry, one could hear terms like 'conflict resolution', 'peace talks' and 'diplomacy'.

Sukanya had been part of the so-called women's militia, and if nothing else, the whole exercise had led to women's emancipation in an unprecedented way. Though women in Kashmir had always been 'free' to make their choices and Kashmiri society had always treated them liberally compared to the rest of the subcontinent, their training in arms had opened up new avenues for them in terms of education and careers. But separatist sentiments had forced Hindu women into wearing bindis and Muslim women into burqas and hijabs. Living in constant fear of the gun meant an increase in the number of girl dropouts from schools due to the violence and uncertainty.

Sukanya's Kashmir was also the land that had nurtured women like Malika Pukhraj, the doyenne of Hindustani classical music who had blossomed in the court of Maharaja Hari Singh. This was the land of *pather bhand,* the folk theatre that is an amalgam of dance, drama, mime, puppetry and music. All its performances end with the recitation of the *dua-e-kher,* a prayer for the betterment of the land and its people and seeking protection from disease and death. Suddenly, listening to music and indulging in any kind of art, especially performing arts, had become vulgar and against Islam in this land.

In Sukanya's Kashmir, Muslim men were tied *rakhis* by their Hindu sisters. In the Kashmir of today, Hindus were still struggling to come out of the camps and find the remnants of a life led with self-respect in a past they were unable to forget. And, for lack of a better and more plausible reason, they blamed the Muslims for it.

Almost a week after Sukanya's death, I was attending a prayer service in her memory, and for a brief moment, the gathering did seem like Sukanya's Kashmir. Both Hindus and Muslims had come to remember their old friend and benefactor who had personified all that was good and beautiful in Kashmir: its Kashmiriyat. I had taken this opportunity to bring Zainab, Zooni and Ananya together. It did seem selfish to use this occasion for my own interests, but I knew Sukanya would not have objected to it. Rather, she would have been proud of me. The setting was perfect: Hindu and Muslim women were meeting at the demise of a Hindu woman who had wanted, more than anything else, for the two communities to coexist, like in old times.

The venue of the first women's workshop meeting where Jehanara, Rafiqa and Ananya had met had been the charming Nishat Bagh. Though the meeting had seen a clash of differing perspectives, it had set the ground for what the women's initiative would be like. The setting was very different for the second meeting, and I was hoping it would be an exchange of viewpoints.

Zooni had lived with Sukanya in her house, and had literally grown up under her tutelage. Zainab had often met Sukanya as part of the academic circle in Kashmir. Sukanya had retired as the principal of the Women's College, and though Zainab had never been her student, she had benefitted immensely from her guidance. For Ananya, Sukanya had been a name to reckon with. Both women, in their own respective ways, symbolized Kashmiri women's liberation and it was only to be expected that they had known each other intimately. For all of us, not having Sukanya amidst us was something we had still not come to terms with. After offering our prayers at the condolence ceremony, we sat in a huddled group. Not surprisingly, there was nothing and no one else other than Sukanya we could reminisce about.

Since Zooni was the one who had spent the maximum time with her, I encouraged her to share her experiences. She recounted how Sukanya had once spoken to a group of boys who were going to join the Students Liberation Front (SLF), the students' wing of the Jammu Kashmir Liberation Front (JKLF). These boys had seen young men from different villages go across the border to receive arms training. The men would come back to their respective villages and would roam around talking to the village folk, visiting schools, eating with everyone, and creating havoc in the daily humdrum of normal life by stirring the Azaadi sentiment and painting a rosy picture of the Pakistan dream. In their military fatigues, the fashion statement of those times, and their Kalashnikovs hanging casually by their sides, the men were worshipped like war heroes. Enamoured by their larger-than-life images, the boys had wanted to follow in their footsteps. So after everyone in the neighbourhood had gone to sleep, the boys would meet outdoors, secretly, in the cover of darkness and plan their escapades. After word spread around and the families got to know what their sons were planning to do, they approached Sukanya, desperate for her help.

Sukanya had called the seven boys to her house. They were of course petrified at the thought of what awaited them. After they had all assembled, Sukanya had treated them to chicken curry and rice and topped it off with some rose-water flavoured *shireen*. Just as the boys were beginning to feel comfortable, she said, 'Until you join the SLF, do come to my house and eat your meals with me every day. Because once you have gone across the border, who knows what kind of a life you will be living? Who knows whether you will get enough food to eat or not? Because in a war, nobody lives for long.' Needless to say, the boys abandoned all ideas about rebellion. Their families thanked Sukanya profusely, who made it a point to have the boys over at least once a week and along with food for their hungry stomachs, also give them food for their hungry souls. The boys had grown up to be fine young men, and were present at the prayer service. We couldn't help but smile.

Zainab's experiences of being with Sukanya had been profound. She had been visiting Kunan Poshpora much before the 'mass rape', which is probably why her presence in the aftermath of the incident was accepted, even if it was not always welcome. One such evening, Sukanya was in the headman's house, and a group of women had come to meet her. The atmosphere was tense, as the incident was fresh in everyone's mind. No one knew what to say and to whom in particular. As the evening light began to fade, the headman's wife started covering all the windows in the house with thick blankets, and she was soon assisted by the other women. When Sukanya asked her why, the headman's wife told her that the security forces personnel, when they came for their daily rounds, would not be able to make out people in the house were still awake because of the blankets. 'We have been forced to extinguish all lights in our homes and hearths, in all our lives,' Sukanya was told.

Sukanya had replied, 'But what about the lights in your heart, and the hearts of every woman in this village? Hearts that beat for their men and children; hearts that beat for the land and its people; hearts that beat for the Kashmiriyat that is fading away; and hearts that beat sometimes for the women themselves – how will you extinguish those lights? And do you even want to do that?' Zainab recalled an uncomfortable silence that had spread about the room; a silence broken by Sukanya's soothing words encouraging the women to pick up the broken pieces of their lives and start all over yet again. We marvelled at the miracle Sukanya was; somehow, she knew the exact words to say to anyone and at any occasion, no matter what the situation or circumstances.

Ananya and Sukanya had first met at a women's conference in Delhi about two years ago. Though the theme of the conference had been something else, the conversation moved towards an encounter at Srinagar's Lal Chowk the previous day. It was neither unusual nor unexpected; it was, however, tragic and appalling. It resulted, amongst other things, in the smashing of the faint hope that everything was slowly 'getting back to normal'. The peace and quiet of the past few months turned out to be the proverbial lull in the storm as the encounter was followed by a daredevil attack on a police station in Sopore, the apple town of Kashmir, which had already been burnt down several times in the past. There were reports that militants had used pre-paid SIM cards despite the fact that they had officially been banned in the state. While reporting on the Lal Chowk encounter, one of the national dailies had published a front-page photograph of a security personnel removing the dead body of a colleague who had died in the cross-firing between the militants and the security forces. There was fire all around; the street was deserted but for a huge vehicle parked in the middle of the road, from under which the dead body was being dragged away.

Naturally, everyone at the conference was expressing their pent-up emotions against the security forces: how cruel they had been; how many lives, mostly civilian and innocent, they had taken; and so on. Sukanya's calm and composed reaction had been: 'I choose to not get into the debate about what the media should publish and what it shouldn't. I also choose to not talk about the ethics of journalism, and how, more often than not, the media moulds events and incidents to make them "jingoistic" and "saleable". Obviously, we haven't learnt the lessons even after the many debates on "appropriate media behaviour" after the Kargil war, the Amarnath agitation and many more such unpleasant occurrences in J&K.

'In fact, what I choose to say here will result in my being labelled as an "agent of India", but I am willing to take the risk. I wish to draw your attention to the thousands of security personnel who are posted in J&K to "protect" the land. Who are they supposed to protect it from and against what is a different issue altogether. For now, let us just take them (the security personnel) to be fellow human beings. Surely they must have families back home who they think of often; there must be football and cricket matches they wish to play; they must have cravings to eat the food they like... So when one of them dies, let us simply bow our heads in empathy and wish for strength and support for their families and friends. It is not for us to sit in judgment.'

Ananya recalled how her anger at the security forces had melted away in the humanitarian light that Sukanya had described them in. In that moment, I was reminded of the many security personnel who I had interacted with over the course of my work. I couldn't deny the fact that I had been helped and supported in my endeavours by the security forces many times. They endured the most inhospitable weather conditions, amongst other things, in the line of duty. I had tried to imagine a life of solitude for months at a stretch on the Siachen glacier with sub-zero temperatures and virtually nothing for company! I couldn't go too far… And somehow, I found these memories of mine quite in contrast to all the dreadful stories I heard about how security forces treated Kashmiri men and women.

It was probably during our third or fourth meeting that Sukanya had suggested we go for a shikara ride. We decided to board the shikara from Dal gate, and go up to the *char-chinari* point on the lake, a small island that has four chinar trees. I remember we were talking about the women's initiative; my vision for it; the difference of opinion between the conference organizers and my own views on Kashmir, etc. I had been a bit troubled, and sensing it, Sukanya had said: 'Move forward with unimpeachable integrity in all that you ever do, and your journey will be one of honesty to both yourself and those whom you will inevitably touch as you move through life.' This was a lesson we can all use and benefit from.

As we bade each other goodbyes after the prayer service, there was a strange but comfortable silence which I was hoping to nurture into fruitful thoughts for the women's conference, all backed by Sukanya's absent support.

My favourite haunt in Srinagar city is Pari Mahal, a garden palace located at the top of the Zabarwan range. It consists of six terraces and offers a panoramic view of the valley. The ruins of an observatory built by Dara Shikoh, the mystic son of the

Mughal emperor Shah Jehan, the gardens were used for teaching astronomy and astrology.

I visited Pari Mahal the morning after Sukanya's prayer service. I wanted some quiet and peace and the solitude offered by this historical setting was just right. I wandered around aimlessly for some time before settling at a spot. I could see a group of women having an animated conversation; they looked like Gujjar women to me, and amidst them was an extremely attractive, city-bred young woman, as was obvious from her clothes and mannerisms. I observed the group for some time, and it was clear that they were bound to each other, and the connecting thread was the young woman. I couldn't help but overhear parts of their conversation, which revolved around embroidery, fabric, colours and the like. Curiosity got the better of me, and I went up to the group and introduced myself. The women were amused, yet welcoming. The young lady introduced herself to me as Roshan.

From an affluent family, as was obvious, Roshan worked with a group of Pahari/Gujjar women who had been trained in basic stitching and tailoring, and when she coupled that with their expertise at embroidery, the products they created were a sell-out. Roshan had carefully and tediously carved out a niche market for the women's products – exquisitely hand-embroidered bags, dupattas, head scarves, shawls, wallets, chappals etc.

I sat with the women as a silent observer, while they went about discussing marketing strategies, reflecting over new trends, arguing about prices and contemplating whether family life was better before or after they started earning their own money. Amidst all this hullabaloo, they made it a point to let Roshan know it was about time she got married, a suggestion Roshan had clearly heard many times before and dismissed with a mere shrug of the shoulders. After bidding the women farewell, she then invited me to join her as she was going into town to meet Jahanavi, a friend of hers.

As we sat waiting for Jahanavi to come, Roshan and I exchanged brief notes on our lives. Roshan's family was one of those long-standing, elitist families of the valley whose presence was as old and as taken for granted as the mountains of Kashmir! Running a chain of hotels along the tourist circuit in Kashmir, and with several business arrangements across the world, the family was a name to reckon with. While Roshan was aware of the privileges of being part of such a family, she was also extremely conscious of the family's social position and its ability to use that very position to contribute towards the growth of her society. She managed a part of the hotel business for her family, simultaneously working with Gujjar women of the area and helping them place themselves somewhat better vis-à-vis their respective families as well as the society at large.

Roshan had chosen to put the issue of her marriage on the backburner for two major reasons: one, she was not willing to put aside all her work and jump into matrimony, not knowing how it would turn out to be; also, she did not know whether she would have the time and space to carry on with the same work post-marriage. The second reason was that she was yet to meet a man willing to understand and accept her passion and devotion to her work, and who would give her work its due respect and recognition in their lives.

On this note, Jahanavi made her entry into the café where we had parked ourselves for the afternoon. Young, vibrant and beautiful, she greeted Roshan with the warmth of an old friend and welcomed my presence in the true spirit of Kashmiriyat. When I asked Jahanavi about herself, she suggested that Roshan and I come with her to her workplace, but not before we had finished a hearty meal since Jahanavi had come to meet us during her lunch break.

Driving along the Dal lake, just when winter was making way for summer and intermittent rain made the valley look ethereal, we reached the polo grounds. J&K has the distinction of having the world's highest polo ground. Ironically, the world's highest battlefield, Siachen, is also in J&K. Jahanavi announced, to no one in particular, that we had arrived at her workplace. Roshan told me she was the manager of the grounds, and this pleasantly surprised me. I suddenly had a mental image of Jahanavi taking charge of the grounds, giving instructions for the upkeep and maintenance, managing high-end events and dealing with the administrative aspect of it. I couldn't help but look at the enterprising woman in awe. She told me it was no easy task, considering she had faced a lot of opposition on many fronts to come to this point.

I considered this casual meeting with Roshan and Jahanavi as my formal introduction to the new breed of Kashmiri women, who not only knew how to take matters in their own hands but also how to deal with those matters, whether related to their personal lives and families or the wider spectrum of societal consciousness. These 'modern' women knew what their preferences in life were; what's more, they even knew what options and choices to make, and what rights to exercise; they knew their minds well; and when to speak their mind and when to remain silent.

Almost on cue, Jahanavi ushered us to her well-kept office, the interiors of which were plush, and gave the impression of being occupied by a person who treated that space with respect and used it with intellect. She showed me with great pride her collection of books. I noted with amusement that she had, in her collection, quite a few books on J&K. She picked up a book and made me read an extract which she had underlined[44]:

> The political and public perceptions of Kashmir vary at the levels of the Indian state and the Indian individual. For most Indians, Kashmir is an exotic place, unreal and wholly imaginary. In the time-honoured manner of stereotyping, the Kashmiris are not seen as real people, they are the 'other'; represented to suit the self-image of mainstream Indians. In the pendulum swing between Bollywood movies and Islamophobia, typically, Kashmir is either filled with an entire assortment of enchanting people and precious things (rosy-cheeked fair girls, apples, walnuts) or a dangerous place filled with repugnant, ungrateful and violent Muslims and almost-Muslims.
>
> But this 'wrecked paradise' of Kashmir is inhabited by real people with real lives and aspirations. The longer India occupies Kashmir instead of understanding what the people there want, the more it will pave the way for the influence of hard-line intolerance in the valley. Already, a land with famous women poetesses like Lalla Ded and

Habba Khatoon is becoming known for women like Asiya Andrabi, the head of the Dukhtaran-e-Millat, or Daughters of the People, which seeks to promote compulsory veiling for women and attempts to enforce rigid Islamic values hitherto alien in Kashmir's syncretic culture.

I wondered whether she was contemplating my stand vis-à-vis Kashmir or was putting forth her own point of view. As the Polo Grounds staff served us refreshing *kahwa*, Jahanavi, Roshan and I debated the present-day status of women in Kashmir. I told them about my brief meeting with Sheeba Umar Farooq and Saima Farhad. While the former is a shy, ordinary Kashmiri whose status is extraordinary (whether she likes it or not) considering she is the wife of the current Mirwaiz, Maulvi Umar Farooq, the latter teaches Sociology at Kashmir University. The two decided to start Kashmir's first all-women's magazine, *She*. The first issue of the magazine came out in April 2006 and had clear feminist undertones. The inaugural edition dealt with teenage dating, breast feeding and other issues a modern working woman faces. While the novelty of the subject of the magazine was unusual for Kashmiris, unfortunately, it didn't go any further than the first issue. The reasons could be several: the magazine and the issues it dealt with were too bold; there were political repercussions which were too volatile to handle; or there were no sponsors who were willing to take the challenge to support it.

The two women – Sheeba and Saima – had dared to embark on a journey which they would have known would be a lonely and brief one. I had tried to meet them again after that one brief encounter. Sheeba's phone would keep ringing, but was never answered. All attempts to reach her through other sources and contacts failed as well. Perhaps she was forced to go underground, and had to put an end to all social meetings and interactions. All I remember of her is that she seemed like a very docile, sweet and homely girl as opposed to the heavy-duty image of her in my mind. She had a strange accent which made her presence in the heavily guarded house of the Mirwaiz almost surreal. When she answered my questions on women in Kashmir, she was sure of what she was saying and had a definite point of view, which surely came from awareness and education. Saima, too, had not been very forthcoming when I suggested we meet again. Her reasons must have been the same. She was more outspoken than Sheeba, and like her, had a point of view which was backed by experience and exposure.

The magazine's discontinuation was unfortunate not just because its non-publication prevented Kashmiri women from having a platform to voice their opinions. It was deplorable because its halt outlined the extremist, hardline nature of a society that had been forced to develop such an attitude to satisfy sinister political aspirations of India and Pakistan.

While the state and Central governments have continued to take measures they thought were appropriate for J&K (Kashmiris and well-meaning individuals across the world may not have approved of those measures), there was an immense abyss in the land itself, in the lives of its people and everything associated with it. This chasm was then sought to be filled by NGO institutions; Kashmir was subsequently introduced to a new term: civil society intervention. There were many things which came to be associated with this new outfit, personal and political agendas and money laundering being just two of them:

> Indian civil society groups have tried to identify or create their respective constituencies by promoting various sub-marginalities. Since funding to NGOs is channelled through the Indian elite, largely based in Delhi, they exercise substantial influence on how 'civil society' in its NGO avatar develops in Kashmir. The initiatives currently active in Kashmir have diverse ideological backgrounds. If we leave out the covert intelligence operations dressed in the form of NGOs, we can site at least three: the Gandhian, the left-leaning, and the feminist. Each sees the central problem in Kashmir to be that of fissuring of the community due to communalism/violence, feudalism and/or patriarchy respectively. While these faultlines exist, to see them as detached from the nationality question does violence to Kashmir. This is akin to British colonialists delegitimizing the Indian nationalist struggle on account of India's backwardness, male chauvinism or caste oppression.[45]

Again, it has been the women who have stood up to confront all that has been happening in the lives of Kashmiris – women like Parveena Ahangar, chairperson of the Association of Parents of Disappeared Persons (APDP); and social activists like Neerja Mattoo and Nighat Shafi Pandit – all have been affected by the turmoil in one way or the other. But rather than succumbing to the circumstances, they have fought back, and all along, they have encouraged and supported countless other women to not give up. Similar women like Roshan and Jahanavi, who defied the stereotypes for women; Sheeba and Saima, who took the bull by its horns; Mehbooba Mufti and Shabnam Ghani Lone, who dared to step into the volatile field of politics; Anuradha Jamwal Bhasin, a journalist and editor whose work speaks of flawless uprightness; Dr Girija Dhar and Krishna Misri, former chairpersons of the Kashmir Women's Commission; Sudha Koul, the first woman IAS officer from the valley; Sushma Chowdhary, the first woman IAS officer from Jammu and many others who braved the circumstances to make their place in the modern history of J&K. What these women have also done is to alter the subconscious of a deeply scarred society. The women's attitudes and exemplary behaviour, whether at work or at home, have been a healing balm, spreading slowly yet steadily, to soothe the troubles.

Contrast this with my meeting with Syed Ali Shah Geelani. When I reached his residence, guarded by heavily armed men, his secretary was highly suspicious of my motives for meeting the hard-line separatist leader. He finally seemed satisfied after several questions, but made it a point to be present for the entire duration of the meeting. In between, his mobile rang to the tune of the national anthem of Pakistan, 'Qaumi Tarana'.

I asked Geelani about the status of women in Kashmir, and his comment was telling: 'The respect and honour bestowed on women by Islam is unparalleled. No "ism" in the world can compare to that – nationalism, socialism or communalism. Islam respects women as women. It does not grant women the status of men – that is not respecting women. The call for feminism is not for liberating women. It is a call to grant women the status of men. I was reading in the newspapers that in America, there are 15 lakh children whose fathers are unknown. If you call such a society liberated, and say that such a society respects women, I don't know what to say!'

Talking of liberated women and societies, I was to meet with Firoza and Sophia, friends of Roshan and Jahanavi. Firoza worked as a senior sub-editor with one of the local leading English dailies and Sophia was an aspiring candidate for the Kashmir Public Services Commission, J&K's civil services competitive examinations. I met them at Residency Road, from where we made our way to my favourite (and one of the very few) coffee shops in town, Café Arabica. As we settled with our respective coffees, Firoza said, by way of introduction: 'There are two cricket matches being played today – one of India and another of Pakistan. I have just told them to make the Pakistan match the lead of the sports pages. I have no choice. My readers want to read this news. If I don't play up the Pakistan match, they will not read me. This is the situation here.' Clad in a pair of jeans and a khadi kurta, her 'journalist' look was complete with a sling bag and glasses that rested on her hair.

Sophia, petite and shy, and dressed immaculately in a salwar-kameez with detailed Kashmiri embroidery, needed a bit of coaxing to open up. To my question as to why she wanted to be a part of the civil services, she answered in a very profound and thoughtful way, 'The voice of Kashmiri people is not unanimous; it does not even approach a consensus. There is a perceptible groundswell in favour of independence, but Kashmiris are aware of the difficulties. Most Kashmiri leaders now concede that the interests of neither India nor Pakistan can be ignored and these interests do not allow for an independent state, which could become a hotbed of international rivalry and intrigue. In the hearts of Kashmiris, the Pakistan dream may have faded away, but it has most definitely not been replaced by a merger with India. I want to work with the people on the ground, ease their confusion and tension and hopefully make Kashmir a better place to live in.'

Firoza was quick to add, 'We have to make compromises at every stage. Look at my newspaper; sometimes we have to fine-tune the content so that we keep getting advertisements. But we have to strike a fine balance each time, for each story. It is a difficult task running a newspaper in Srinagar. Earlier, militants used to directly call us to complain. And we possibly could not ignore security forces either. These days, this has become less frequent. But one has to be aware and alert at all times.'

As we were talking, we were joined by Roshan and Jahanavi, with another vivacious woman who had 'rebellion' written all over her. She was introduced to me as Aliya, and I was told she was beginning to create ripples in the art circles of Kashmir. She was a painter, and her forte, according to her, was surrealism. Dividing her time between Kashmir, New Delhi, Mumbai and London, Aliya was the complete antithesis of every single Kashmiri woman I had met till then. Right from her sense of dressing, obviously influenced by her exposure and experiments with life, to the way she talked and conducted herself, Aliya was a bizarre mix of ethnicity and modernism.

Sitting with these five women – Roshan, Jahanavi, Firoza, Sophia and Aliya – who defined the modern Kashmiri woman, I was having difficulties reconciling to all that I had seen and experienced in Kashmir over the past decade. This new breed of self-made, independent Kashmiri women knew their minds well and were not only capable of making their own decisions, but would also not have it any other way.

I took this opportunity and set about giving them a brief on the women's initiative and the conference, and skeletal sketches of my seven special women – Sukanya, Zooni, Rafiqa, Ananya, Jehanara, Zainab and Sonam. I said it aloud, and to no one in particular, that it would be wonderful if the five were a part of the conference as well, maybe not as active participants, but most certainly as a representation of Kashmiri women in the twenty-first century! I made a mental note of chalking out their roles and participation in the conference in the peace and solitude of my room in Rasheed's houseboat.

Bringing me back to the present, Sophia said, again very philosophically, 'All Kashmiris place primary emphasis on personal security and want an end to the bloodshed. All Kashmiris want to be free to travel anywhere in the erstwhile state of J&K without hindrance. All Kashmiris want more autonomy so that they can run their own affairs. All Kashmiris would like to see cooperation between the two parts of the state in fields like tourism, forest management, water and power, and environment. Most Kashmiris welcome improvement in Indo–Pak relations. And this is something which should be highlighted in your conference.'

# Khanaqah & Ziyarat

*Master, leave these palm leaves and birch barks*
*to parrots who recite the name of God in a cage.*
*Good luck, I say, to those who think they've read the scriptures.*
*The greatest scripture is the one that's playing in my head.*[46]

Kashmir's foundations were neither based on religion nor language; the region came together not around a set of ideas about how people should lead their lives, but around a beautiful and holistic concept – 'Kashmiriyat'. Kashmiriyat is what one would call the way of life in the valley, and it has been defined over centuries by an eclectic mix of ideas and cultures, aided by the fact that Kashmir is separated from the rest of the world for almost half the year due to its weather.

The distinctive identity of Kashmir was shaped by multiple influences and rulerships. Kashmir's history

> is a knot of contested interpretations made worse by ignorance. The biggest myth of recent times is that of seeing Kashmir historically in terms of Muslims *versus* Hindus, instead of Muslims *and* Hindus.
>
> Kashmiris did not see themselves in these terms until they were classified as such by the political games of the later part of the twentieth century. The centuries-old tradition of Kashmiriyat bears testimony to the identity of Kashmiris as a people who did not let their religious affiliations overwhelm their ethnic and regional commonality.[47]

In other words, a coexistence and confluence of Islam, Hinduism, Sikhism, Buddhism and Sufism resulted in a typical secular culture which was to become the trademark of Kashmir. As a result, the Kashmir valley evolved its own language, its own food, its own costumes and customs and its own music, myths and folklore.

While it is not unusual for any place, anywhere on the planet, to develop a distinctive identity of its own – owing to specific cultures, customs, and costumes – what was unique about Kashmir's cultural identity was that it was the result of a syncretic mix of Hinduism, Islam, Sikhism, Sufism and Buddhism. The flames of the Bhakti movement further enriched the texture and flavour of Kashmiriyat, where women and men are revered equally. This was a land where Sikhs named the children of their Muslim brethren; where Hindu priests took care of Muslim shrines; where there was no need for separate religious identities – being a Kashmiri defined people's existence and underlined everything there was to life. It was a land where the Kushan emperor Kanishka conducted the fourth Buddhist Council in the first century CE; where waking up to the sound of the azaan was normal. Here, homes were not defined as Hindu or Muslim homes. In both Hindu and Muslim kitchens, fish was fried behind closed doors to keep away unwanted attention and also to ensure the devil was not attracted towards their house. Though Hindu women wore their earrings dangling on a long chain of gold which was pierced through the ears in a typical Pandit fashion and Muslim women wore the hijab and burqa, women from both homes wore the *pheran*, and this defined their identity. It was this Kashmiriyat that came under threat once separatist sentiments got mobilized. Kashmiri separatism has had internal as well as external dimensions. While the external have all emerged out of Pakistan's contestation of J&K and its supposed accession to India, the internal dimensions have been multi-layered – a separatist movement, armed militancy, identity politics, the failure of democracy as a concept, alienation of common Kashmiris from the Indian State, to list a few. Often referred to as heaven on earth, Kashmir is also the most militarized zone in the world, owing to the presence of more than half a million troops even now. Although the internal situation has undergone many changes, the presence of the Army has been a constant.

What has also remained constant is the state and plight of women across the length and breadth of the state. In a broader sense of the term 'civil society', Jammu, Srinagar and Ladakh have had very distinct women's groups. In the Buddhist-majority Leh, organizations such as the Women's Alliance,

Women's Action Committee, Women's Centre and Mahila Mandal deal with issues of women's rights after marriage, their representation in local bodies and their status within the family. In Muslim-majority Kargil, women's bodies fight for women's education, health and political representation. In Jammu, where women have been politically passive, there are groups that work in Kashmiri migrant camps on the outskirts of the city. Some other groups engage in imparting stitching and embroidery techniques to women in an effort to make them financially independent. The valley – which is the 'hub' of the Kashmir conflict – has groups like the APDP (Association of Parents of Disappeared Persons), the HELP (Human Effort for Love and Peace) Foundation and groups involved in making women financially stable by taking up tailoring etc. There are also organizations that take on research-based work, thereby influencing the lives of Kashmiri women in a strategy-oriented, academic manner.

No doubt the work taken up by these organizations, no matter how minuscule the level of intervention and outreach, has had an impact on women's lives in J&K. Sadly, the common thread running through all such organizations in the three regions is the lack of a politically motivated will to speak up and fight for their rights, both personal as well as political. This is not an easy task in a place like J&K, where for more than half the population – especially women – the most challenging task of the day is to organize the next meal for their families.

I often ask myself why women in Kashmir in the twenty-first century are unaware of their rights in a place where the National Conference encouraged the formulation of a so-called 'women's militia' as early as in 1947? The official peace process in India, when it comes to Kashmir, has often forgotten to include women as equal partners, leaving their positions even more unstable and suspended. This is despite women being at the helm of affairs when it comes to 'constructing peace' in a war-torn society like Kashmir – pulling communities together and building bridges for reconstructing lives.

While militants and security forces have targeted women in the most brutal ways – Dardpora and Kunan Poshpora are just two examples – the governments, both state and Central, have either ignored women in their rehabilitation schemes and relief packages, or done little towards re-settling their lives. In such a scenario, the onus is on civil society organizations to strongly take up the cause of women. While most groups remain engaged with children, families of militants, families of disappeared persons, health issues, environment and handicrafts etc., there are very few that engage directly with women's issues.

> ...For them (women), most conflicts remain above all devastating experiences, marked by gross atrocities and large-scale human rights violations such as sexual violence, rape, and forced prostitution. Hence, while discussing the management of the process of women's agency in violent conflict, one must perpetually keep in mind the uneasy tension between vulnerability and victimhood on one hand, and empowerment and emancipation on the other, always resisting the impulse to prioritize the one over the other.[48]

One of the reasons why we find the women of J&K in this present state could be because of the lack of an organized women's movement towards stabilizing the position of women in Kashmiri society. It is a well-known fact that Kashmiri women are skilled workers, whether it is the home front or the agricultural field; whether it is papier mache or crewel embroidery. However, there is nothing that the women do for themselves, nothing whatsoever to establish their own identity as women.

One of the themes I have repeatedly explored over the years within the scope of my work with Kashmiri women is their 'Azaadi'. As Angana Chatterji says, 'Azaadi' can represent many things across rural and urban spaces in J&K, yet these multiple meanings are steadfastly united in that freedom *always* signifies an end to India's authoritarian governance.[49] The context for each Kashmiri woman's freedom may be different, however; it could mean different things to different women – for example, freedom from the fear of living under the shadow of the gun; freedom from the constant worry of whether their family members will return home safely; freedom from having to stress about where the next meal will come from; freedom of expression; freedom to express displeasure over the state of affairs; freedom to live in the valley and practice one's faith; freedom to travel the length and breadth of the world and not be identified as a Kashmiri, and therefore 'dangerous'! All these different desires for freedom lead to one thing: freedom from Indian governance.

Sukanya, Ananya, Zooni, Rafiqa, Jehanara, Zainab and Sonam – I travelled with each one of them on the journeys of their respective lives, to understand them as stakeholders in Kashmir, and more crucially, as women who were unique, considering their individual backgrounds, circumstances and life experiences.

Sukanya Parashar, the epitome of grace and elegance, came from a happy childhood and had an adolescence full of excitement and uncertainty. Her middle years were spent experiencing events that were unusual for women in that day and age. During the days I spent with her, I could almost live, breathe and experience her Azaadi through her recollection of events during the 1947 invasion. That episode defined Sukanya's existence. I could almost imagine how, for her, everything would have revolved around that single affair, and thereafter, everything would have been coloured by the event. What I admired about Sukanya was that she never allowed herself to get carried away by the memories of 1947. She lived her life in the present and made the most of everything. Even in her death, she inspired all those around her to do the same.

It was the same fire that I sensed in Zooni. A rebel not just in her family, but in the entire region of Kulali–Marrah, she first fell in love with a militant. Then, when things got out of hand and she could no longer control her life, she chose to leave her village and go with Sukanya to live in the city. As Zooni and I had wandered about Kulali–Marrah on our visit there, I felt that she regretted neither of her two decisions. She had managed to define the course of her life through these events at a very early age and she seemed to be relishing the liberation they brought along.

For Ananya Bhat, the meanderings of life were her Azaadi. She did go through traumatic and unsettling events in her childhood, and those events helped her become the person that she grew up to be. Her uprooting from the valley and the events thereafter, the opportunity to travel abroad, estrangement from her family and community, and finally her being able to find acceptance and eventually establish an individualistic space for herself through her book and her women's platform *Voices*, it was a long, tumultuous journey, but one that she thoroughly took pleasure and pride in!

Rafiqa introduced me to a new term that I struggle to understand even today – 'half-widow'. Her beauty and charisma surpassed everything else around her. Her transition from a chirpy young girl to that of a sombre woman whose eyes defined pain was not just difficult but also laden with danger. She defied the norm by making contact with several militant groups to trace her husband. The price she had to pay for it was heavy, but in her own words, at least her family would not be able to say she had left anything undone.

Jehanara put aside her personal life, or whatever was left of it, and absorbed everyone who came along in it. There wasn't a single family in the valley untouched by her, either physically or through the work she did with those whose men had gone missing. It seemed this was the only way she knew how to live her life. Whether she called it the only way to divert herself from her personal misfortune of losing her son or whether she called it her own Azaadi was not clear to me, but in either case, her courage and integrity was awe-inspiring.

Zainab's name could be synonymous with tragedy. As if being violated as a woman was not enough, she was repeatedly reminded of the mishap either by circumstances or by people like myself who treated her and others like her as objects of study for their own interests. To deal with life in the aftermath of the Kunan Poshpora rapes, Zainab found courage within her. There was no support forthcoming from any front, and this painful realization and the strength therefore to rely on none other than herself would surely have been her liberation.

Sonam had always fended for herself. The way things were, she would continue to do so for as long as she lived. Extending support came naturally to her, whether it was for her daughter's children or for the community at large, as was very clear from her involvement with relief and rehabilitation work in the aftermath of the cloudburst. Her resilience and never-say-die attitude towards life was what I would call her Azaadi, and each event of hardship simply reinforced it and made her a wee bit stronger each time.

All of them, except Sukanya, were to meet the following week. I had also extended the invitation for the women's workshop to Roshan, Jahanavi, Firoza, Sophia and Aliya. Some of these women had met each other before, and some had not, but all of them knew about the others since we had been talking about each other all the time. We would all miss Sukanya's presence immensely. None of us expected the meeting to be a smooth exchange of ideas and notions. But for whatever it would turn out to be, we were anxious to get started.

Personally, for me, bringing together this diverse group of women was enriching in every sense of the word. I couldn't help but compare some of the events in my own life with those of my women. More than anything else, this time-consuming exercise helped me explore my very own Azaadi.

Like Agha Shahid Ali wrote in his poem 'Postcard from Kashmir':

> Kashmir shrinks into my mailbox,
> my home a neat four by six inches
> I always loved neatness. Now I hold
> the half-inch Himalayas in my hand.

I am often asked what drew me to research in J&K. I usually have a long answer for it, but the crux lies in the diversity of the so-called 'Kashmir problem'. The complexities at every step of life in J&K allow for so much to be explored (not necessarily good for those living there!), and despite years of working in the area, I still feel I don't know enough. The Jammu–Kashmir–Ladakh divide does not really help to clear things. While the valley has received a lot of international attention, aid, civil society intervention and media coverage (justifiably so), Jammu and Ladakh seem to have been caught in murky regional politics.

Unfortunately, while the two capital cities of Srinagar and Jammu remain entangled in debates, arguments, accusations, controversies and land rows, and Ladakh continues to feel ignored and sidelined, the Kashmir conflict remains largely unaddressed in inaccessible districts and villages of J&K. For example, in village Tarkundi, sandwiched between the border districts of Poonch and Rajouri, 90 per cent of its residents had migrated due to heavy cross-border shelling and firing, but an election booth was set up for the remaining two families which chose to stay back; Salhotri, the last Indian village in Poonch from where on a clear morning, one can 'see' a Pakistani mosque and a Pakistani engineering college just across, all the houses have their gates and entrances facing the opposite direction because you never know when a shell might land in your courtyard!

When I started visiting Kashmir a decade ago, the undercurrent was still very tense and sensitive, though nothing compared to the situation of the early '90s. My beloved travel companion, Hussain, would pick me up from the airport and drop me at Welcome Hotel on the Boulevard, with strict instructions to me and to the hotel staff to not allow me to venture out after six in the evening. He even went to the extent of introducing me to a friend of his who owned a shikara, and I was to take a shikara ride on the beautiful Dal Lake with no one other than Hussain's trusted friend, Ilyas. The hours for that excursion were also fixed, obviously, by Hussain. And of course, he himself would drive me wherever I needed to go.

During my first few visits to Srinagar, things were tense; even a ten-year-old could narrate the history and events of Kashmir as if it were a lesson he or she had learnt in school just the previous day! Very slowly, the situation began to 'normalize', and years later, in 2011, I drove down from Ladakh to Srinagar on my own and by myself, and arrived in the city at midnight. The hotel staff did not even blink at me arriving so late in the night. I wonder if it was due to life returning to 'normal', or their being used to my eccentric ways!

Over the years, I recall having absolutely no fear during my travels, not even when I went to the valley for the very first time. My brief encounters with 'danger', which I like to fondly refer to as 'adventures', were hardly any match for the stories every well-wisher (including family and friends) would feel obligated to narrate to me. The so-called militants, the few that I did meet, were bright, young men who had high-flying notions of liberating their motherland. They were certainly no match for Indian security forces and did not pose any danger to me whatsoever. On the contrary, they were all very polite, almost respectful, in the way they treated me.

Events in the India–Kashmir–Pakistan calendar have no place in the everyday lives of the protagonists of this book and/or other common Kashmiris. But the way their lives have been affected and shaped by these events speaks volumes. Like the elections of 1996, 2002, and 2008: elections that promised the world, but delivered very little; or a fresh round of talks between India and Pakistan, and a new wave of CBMs (confidence-building measures); or the much-feted Agra Summit; or the opening of the Srinagar–Muzaffarabad bus service and the opening of trade routes between the two countries; or terrorist strikes like the IC-814 hijack, the 26/11 attacks in Mumbai – and many more.

Rather, it is people like Firdous Syed Baba, once a hardcore militant who later tried a stint at politics and when disillusioned by that became a fierce peace activist, who have affected Kashmiris the most; or Mirwaiz Umar Farooq, who wanted to study computers but found himself leading Kashmiris as their religious head after his father Mirwaiz Moulvi Farooq was assassinated; or the children of Abdul Ghani Lone: sons Sajjad and Bilal, and daughter Shabnam, who, after a brief spell in politics, seem lost in the murky maze of Kashmir; or Yasin Malik, who, despite his affair with militancy, remains committed to peace. The inability to draw these people into the negotiations on Kashmir shows a huge gap in the official peace process, and this is perhaps the biggest failure on the Indian side.

The even more conspicuous missing link is the inclusion of women who have defined the shape of life and set the trend in many ways during the conflict, but their presence on a formal platform is not even noticed or acknowledged. They have all been affected by the turmoil in one way or the other. Yet, rather than succumb to circumstances, they have stood up and fought back. In the words of journalist Suhasini Haider, '... the Kashmiri movement is not going to die, but it might be coming to terms with the limits of what it can achieve. Azaadi means many things to many people here, but one version of it seems to be about achieving the maximum freedom within the "non-redrawable borders" the Indian leadership refers to.'

I have often wondered about my own liberation; surely the path to my Azaadi has been the path I have travelled on during my innumerable visits to J&K. Sitting on a hillock, I was witness to the night sky in Doda as it was flooded with millions of stars. Down in the valley and on faraway mountains, lights from scattered villages made me feel like I was wrapped in a blanket of stars. This spectacle, however, was punctured every few minutes with the long, swaying and blinding Army searchlights as they pried into every nook and corner of Doda every few minutes. Under the stars and searchlights of Doda, in village Ghat, I have had many discussions and arguments with Hashmi sa'ab, one of my many Abbus in Kashmir, on whether this is what I wanted to do and should be doing with my life:

'wandering' around militant-infested J&K to make sense out of the insanity of peace politics.

On one occasion, a debate was triggered between Abbu and I by my mention of a visit to Suchetgarh, an international border post between India and Pakistan that lies ahead of the Ranjit Singh Pura sector in Jammu. I had special permission, courtesy journalist Rakshpal Dasgotra, to visit the area. The post leads to a huge gate that has the Indian flag painted on it on both sides. As the gate is opened, one can see a similar gate just a few steps away, and technically that is the point from where the territory of Pakistan begins. That gate, obviously, has the Pakistani flag painted on both sides. And this is the international border, which is demarcated by pillars strung together by wires. This particular border is not contested, and both India and Pakistan amicably agree to their respective boundary lines.

One of the pillars along the border is an old and historic banyan tree, as wide and big as a eight-seater dining table. Half the tree falls on the Indian side, and the other half on the Pakistani side. It is very difficult to express what I felt when I touched that banyan tree. No doubt it was a beautiful experience, something that brings tears to my eyes every time I relive it.

I have always contrasted this experience with another visit to one of the border areas – Laroka–Laam in the Nowshera sector. A few miles away from the LoC, when I visited a school here, it was unique to see children sitting out in the open and studying, with no formal set-ups of classrooms and study boards. Though this is not an uncommon sight, especially in most parts of rural India, it was unique in its setting. One of the children took me slightly away from his open-air classroom, and pointing his finger towards the clouds of smoke coming from a distance, he said, 'Do you see the smoke...that is Pakistan...' Quite honestly, I was speechless for a few minutes. When I recovered, I was curious as to what happens when relations between India and Pakistan are tense, and there is shelling and gun-battle in border areas. The answer was quite predictable: 'We have no school! We run away from our villages temporarily and come back when things have settled.'

Both sides of my family hail from the Sindh region in Pakistan. My childhood bedtime stories were of the good old days in Pakistan. I have grown up listening to how life was much simpler and more beautiful in the country now forbidden to me. Viewing the very same Pakistan from across the border as a fuzzy grey area was a strange and weird feeling, to say the least.

Pakistan-sponsored terrorism in J&K has led to the Indian Army building a fence along 734 km of the 742 km-long LoC. Started in the year 2003, the fence was built at a cost of Rs 35 lakhs per kilometre. It comprises twelve-feet high Y-shaped pillars, connected with barbwire, and with concrete flooring and floodlight fittings. The total cost of the fence was a whopping Rs 351 crores.

According to the Army, the fencing has enhanced its capability to detect and intercept infiltration and exfiltration attempts, and acts as an effective deterrent against terrorists. However, Pakistan has, from time to time, claimed that the fencing activity undertaken by India is in violation of the Simla Agreement and the December 1972 Agreement on the delineation of the LoC. Later, I learnt about the thirty-odd villages sandwiched between the LoC and the Indian Army fence!

The decision to build the fence was based on practical matters. It had to follow natural topography and strategic considerations. Construction had begun before the November 2003 Indo–Pak ceasefire, and thus, the jawans involved in its construction were direct targets of Pakistani firing. Work on the fence had to be stopped in between, and was later resumed and completed in late 2004. The area to be fenced was marked keeping in view the fact that soldiers would get necessary cover in the form of small geographical features like hills to avoid casualties. For reasons such as these, the fencing does not exactly coincide with the LoC.

As a result, however, there is a distance of approximately two to three kilometres (at certain points, the distance is more) between the fence and the LoC. And between the two lines are approximately thirty villages, which fall on the Indian side and not in 'No Man's Land'. Some of the villages are: Makri, Seri, Manika Maha Dev, Laam, Kalsian, Jhangar and Bhawani in the Nowshera sector of Rajouri district; Sekhlu area (which has been bifurcated by the LoC), Haveli Assembly segment and Shahpur Panchayat of Poonch district; Hathlanga, Chiranda and Silikut villages of Uri sector of Baramulla district; and Chatkadiyan village (which has been bifurcated by the LoC) in the Tangdhar valley.

When I first chanced upon the fence during my initial years in J&K, my naive mind mistook it for the elusive LoC itself! To me, it was unimaginable that the formidable, ugly fence could be anything else other than the LoC. The fact that these villages are outside the Army's 'protective' fence has given rise to immense problems for the residents of these villages. Since their land has been divided by the fence, they have to traverse long distances just to till their land; the fence can be crossed only through proper gates, located at a distance of 500 metres to a kilometre; the gates open and close at fixed times; and the villagers have to keep their ID cards on their person at all times. There is thorough checking at the various gates, and only after several rounds of checks are the villagers allowed to move about – all these measure are extremely inconvenient and humiliating for the people. Of course, what happens during tense situations between the two countries is a different story altogether! An overwhelming fear exists in the minds of the villagers that if India and Pakistan eventually settle on Kashmir, India will give them away to Pakistan.

I find no better words than those of yet another beloved Abbu in Srinagar to describe how it must be for the villagers: 'A Kashmiri has had to divide his heart into four parts – one for India, one for Pakistan, one for Azaadi, and one which is still confused and does not know what it wants ...' When I mentioned this to my Abbu in Doda, his anger at my supposedly aimless 'wanderings' in Kashmir seemed to diminish. He explained to me the words of Kashmiri poet Abdul Ahad Azad:

*Kudratas byun byun thavvin*
*yod aashan millat th kaum*
*Preth akis byun byun zameena*
*aasmana aasi he*

If God meant to create separate nations and religions,
He would have also created separate skies and
earths for them.

Doda, known to the world as the 'hotbed of militancy in Kashmir', has always boasted communal harmony, and rightly so. There are villages in the district which have a 100 per cent Hindu population, and these families have been living in Doda for ages. A village called Arnora has only Rajputs, believed to be the descendants of the rulers from Rajasthan. Another village, Bhadroon, has a completely Dalit population. Several villages like Kalihand, Bhabnor, Shiva, Dashnan and many more have a mixed population of Hindus and Muslims, living together amicably.

Talking of Hindu–Muslim unity, I had once visited Kheer Bhavani with a friend. This temple, dedicated to the goddess Ragnya Devi (who has many other names as well), is in village Tula Mula, ahead of Srinagar city. Legend has it that the colours of the waters surrounding the little goddess are a prediction of the times to come. My friend and I joined the many Hindus, Muslims and Sikhs in trying to please the goddess with offerings and prayers. During a trip to Jammu, I also happened to go to Baba Buddan Shah's *ziyarat,* again accompanied by another friend. We joined the many Hindus, Muslims and Sikhs simultaneously seeking blessings at the holy shrine. These two visits – the first to a Hindu temple in Muslim-majority valley, and the second to a Sufi shrine in Hindu-majority Jammu – changed the whole connotation of the term 'inter-faith' for me.

The land of J&K, to me, symbolizes diversity and oneness,

as well as discontent and harmony – all at the same time. This is represented by the people as much as by the land itself. In the words of M.J. Akbar[50]:

> This message of harmony created a reservoir of humanism which became the ideological fountainhead of the modern Kashmiri mind, gave a unique quality to the Kashmiri identity, provided a conviction which long preserved Kashmir from the unspeakable and unbelievable bloodshed which Indians have inflicted upon each other in this century in the name of religion. It can only be described as the faith of Kashmir, a faith which has been witnessed by anyone who has visited the valley and had the good sense to see beyond the extraordinary beauty of mountain, lake, forest and glade into something far greater, far more luminous, far more enchanting: the beauty of the Kashmiri heart, the Kashmiri soul.

J&K is also my learning ground. I doubt if there could be another school so rich in the assorted lessons it teaches: lessons in survival, in diversity, in spirituality, and in companionship. And very often, one learns these lessons on the road, literally, through the medium of signposts which are interesting, and at times, amusing!

On a trip to district Poonch, I decided to visit Chakan-da-Bagh. Sentiments had peaked in view of the renewed cross-border trade between the two sides of Kashmir, and there was talk of the exchange of goods being stopped for various political reasons. As I neared the Tourist Reception Centre, there were several signposts high on emotion. One read: *Sarhadein zameen baant sakti hain, dil nahin* (borders can divide lands, not hearts); another said: *Kashmir se Kanyakumari tak Bharat ek hai* (India stands undivided, from Kashmir to Kanyakumari). Then, while travelling from Srinagar to district Ramban, after the Jawahar tunnel, a signpost said: *BEACON – jo chahe kar dikhae; Coca-Cola – enjoy!* Perhaps it was referring to the enormity of the task BEACON, the Border Roads Organization's unit, had accomplished in building something as mammoth as the Jawahar tunnel, a reminder of its undying spirit. In district Rajouri, on my way to Surankote, monkeys lined the road, waiting for kind travellers who might feed them. As if on cue, a signpost appeared: *Dosti – yeh dil maange more.* As a stark reminder of the history of the area as well as the general current scenario in Kashmir, another signpost read: 'Kashmir – neighbour's envy, owner's pride.'

Travelling the roads of J&K has been my personal liberation, and the journey could not have been better! The distinct experiences I have encountered here at every crossroad and turn make Kashmir my holy land, my very own personal Mecca. My journey has seen 'hardcore' militants turn into fierce peace activists and media persons; the smallest of issues becoming raging fires of religious discontent and dispute; the briefest encounters ending up in relationships lasting a lifetime... This journey has also seen me lose precious friends in Kashmir: to illnesses, to bomb blasts, to misunderstandings and confusion. Most crucially, it has been a journey of being lost and then being found, and having found precious friends and families which I can call my very own. In a nutshell, the land of Kashmir is my anchor.

# Acknowledgements

*Lord! I've never known who I really am, or You.*
*I threw my love away on this lousy carcass*
*And never figured it out: You're me, I'm You.*
*All I ever did was doubt: Who am I? Who are you?*[51]

Kashmir: the roof of the world, paradise on earth, the place God made first, where earth meets sky, the land of abundance, the land of apples and apricots, and of beautiful women.

I had, for very long, cherished the dream of writing about Kashmir, about my many experiences with the land and its people. The very first time I set foot in this mystic land, I knew there would be more visits. 'Each night puts Kashmir in your dreams,' Agha Shahid Ali, one of Kashmir's most celebrated poets, had written in one of his poems – 'I See Kashmir from

New Delhi at Midnight'. Working in J&K, I had begun doing that – quite unconsciously – much before I came across Agha's verse.

My visits to Kashmir have yielded a captivating collection of memories, and all of them play themselves over each night in my dreams, in many different forms. Some of them are pleasant recollections; some dark reminders of the trauma the Kashmiri people face on a daily basis. The memories I hold closest to my heart are the ones that have come to me as a result of working closely with the women of Kashmir. This book is largely footnoted to all those women, with whom I've had the privilege of interacting, and therefore strengthening my relationship with Kashmir.

For this cherished dream to turn into reality, I have had the backing of many friends and well-wishers: Patrick, my mentor, without whom I wouldn't have been around; the entire Samarpan Foundation gang, with their unconditional love, support and empathy; my husband, Palash, whose mark is unmistakable; my brother, Hitesh, whose presence has always brightened up the darkest, gloomiest days; my daughter, Mallika, with whom I share a camaraderie that is unmatched; Ma, who has been there for me and has allowed me to take her for granted; my sister-in-law, Preeti, who, in her silent ways, has been supportive; little Dia, who brings immense joy; Dadi ma, who always warmed me with her never-ending love and her stories from Pakistan; and my father and grandfather, who have influenced me greatly.

Thank you Anand, for standing by and indulging me through all the turbulence; Saurabh, for being a friend for all times and seasons; Dr Peters, for bringing me back to life; and Jonathan, for making me re-discover Kashmir and myself. Rita Purvis has always brought a smile to my face, despite the physical distance between us. Preeti Gill and Deepti Priya Mehrotra have supported me in ways they may not even know, as also Suhasini Haider, whose work in and on Kashmir I greatly admire, and has encouraged my own work. Rama, Mark, Shahid, Asif and Uttam have maintained the links. Rajneesh, who I was re-united with in Jammu after ten long years, affectionately coaxed me into writing this book. A special thanks to Mohit for sheltering and nurturing my free spirit.

Dr Ajai Sahni promoted and supported me when I needed it the most; M.J. Akbar guided me over the years; Harsh Mander had immense faith in me and taught me never to give up; Andrew Whitehead introduced me to a different world of Kashmiri women; Basharat Peer's *Curfewed Night* put things in perspective; Zafar Choudhary of *Epilogue* gave me an opportunity to share my experiences with his readers; and Ravi Hemadri trusted me with some of the work at The Other Media. The backing of the Women's Press Corps made a huge difference.

Experiences gained in Kashmir during my associations with Women in Security, Conflict Management and Peace (WISCOMP) and the Centre for Dialogue and Reconciliation (CDR) laid the foundations for this book; the brief scholarship period at the London School of Economics to study 'Democracy and Public Policy', and to intern at Panos London, was wonderful in many ways. It was in London that I met Andy Carl, and thus began my relationship with Conciliation Resources, from which I have benefitted immensely. It was also here that I got the opportunity to compare snow in Kashmir with snow in London. Thereafter, I have never disliked the snow in Kashmir!

A fellowship with the Rajaratnam School of International Studies, Singapore, on 'Non-traditional Security Issues', and with Jagori, a women's resource centre in New Delhi, helped a great deal with groundwork and research – my gratitude to colleagues at both institutions for allowing me to use parts of the research as the basis for some of the text in this book. The unparalleled experience of working in Ladakh in the aftermath of the 2010 cloudburst, building pre-fabricated houses for flood victims with the Samarpan Foundation, has deeply influenced me and this book.

A special mention about the idyllic peace and solitude provided by the monsoons in Goa, where a major part of the writing of this book happened. Also, the remote wilderness of the Sunderbans was a dream come true, despite the tough working conditions.

Friends and colleagues (and their families) in J&K are too many to be named here. I would want each one of them to know that they have made me feel 'at home': Nighat ji, Sheikh Mushtaq, Fayaz Kabli, Haroon, Sarwar, Ezabir, Pawan, Sapna, Navreet, Sanjay Dhar, Asim, and many more! Pinto and Tsering Narboo, Namgyal Angchuk, and Thinles Namgyal and his family, encouraged all the work in Ladakh. The Amla family in Srinagar has always been supportive and welcoming. Friends from the 'other side' of the border helped me deconstruct my notions of people from the 'other side'. Thank you all for making me, a 'non-Kashmiri', a part of your lives and world.

Thank you Urmila, Binita, Mayna, Dipen, Surjay, Ajay, Binod and Santok for keeping the kitchen fires burning, and maintaining the warmth and comfort of 'home'.

My deepest gratitude to my editor, Amish, for sorting out a rather confused and jumbled mass of words, and bringing it to its present form. A big 'thank you' to the entire Hachette India team for their support and encouragement towards this maiden effort of mine. Thanks also to Shivmeet Deol who helped with the initial hitches. A special mention of Pooja Mertia, Saffron Design, for the stunning book cover. Thank you Renu Rao, for proofing the text of this book.

Lalla would know that I humbly invoke her presence at the beginning of each section in this book, as in everyday life. And if Agha Shahid Ali could read this book, he would know I took his words very seriously!

# Bibliography

## *Books*


Ranjit Hoskote (trans.); *I, Lalla: The Poems of Lal Ded*; Penguin; 2011

Holger Kersten; *Jesus Lived in India: His Unknown Life Before and After the Crucifixion*; Element; 1994

Sudha Koul; *The Tiger Ladies: A Memoir of Kashmir;* Review; 2002

M.J. Akbar; *Kashmir: Behind The Vale;* Roli Books; 2002

Navnita Chadha Behera; *Demystifying Kashmir*; The Brookings Institution; 2006

S. Gupta; *Kashmir: A Study in India Pakistan Relations;* Asia Publishing House; 1996

Justice A. S. Anand; *Development of the Constitution of Jammu and Kashmir,* Light and Life; 1980

Alistar Lamb; *Kashmir: A Disputed Legacy 1846-1990*; Oxford Books; 1991

Malika Pukhraj; *Song Sung True: A Memoir;* Kali for Women; 2003

Helena Norberg-Hodge; *Ancient Futures: Learning from Ladakh*; Sierra Club Books; 1991

Sanjay Kak (edited.); *Until My Freedom Has Come: The New Intafada in Kashmir*; Penguin; 2011

Urvashi Butalia (edited); *Speaking Peace: Women's Voices from Kashmir;* Kali for Women; 2002

Wajahat Habibulah; *My Kashmir: Conflict and the Prospects of Enduring Peace*; United States Institute of Peace Press; 2008

Alex Austin, Martina Fischer & Norbert Ropers (edited.); *Transforming Ethnopolitical Conflict: The Berghof Handbook*; VS-Verlag; 2004

## *Journals*

*Economic and Political Weekly of India*; June 1990

*Washington Quarterly* 24, No. 2; Spring 2001

*Faultlines: Writings on Conflict & Resolution*, Vol. 18, January 2007 and Vol. 19, April 2008

(Some text in the 'Introduction' section has been taken from my paper 'Jammu and Kashmir: Women's Role in the post-1989 Insurgency', published in *Faultlines* in April 2008. It has been used here with the permission of the journal's editor, Dr Ajai Sahni.)

## *Magazines*

*Himal*; November/ December 1996 and March 2011

(Some text for the Ladakh segment in the section 'Humsaya & Boonye' has been taken from my article 'After the Cloudburst', published in *Himal* in March 2011. The text has been used with the permission of the magazine.)

*Realpolitik*; November 2007

(Some text for the wedding description in the section 'Humsaya & Boonye' has been taken from the article 'A Wedding in Kashmir', written by my husband, Palash Kumar, published in *Realpolitik*; November 2007. The text has been used here with the permission of the magazine's editor, Shahid Faridi. Some names in the text have been changed to protect identities.)

*Epilogue*; 2009–2010

(Some text in the various sections of the book has been taken from my columns in the magazine *Epilogue*, in the years 2009 and 2010. It has been used here with the permission of its editor, Zafar Choudhary.)

## *Websites*

http://freepresskashmir.com/kashmirs-half-widows-seethe-in-bloody-conflict-061114/

http://www.guardian.co.uk/global-development/2010/oct/11/1

http://www.svabhinava.org/abhinava/YoginderSikand/MuslimRishis-frame.php

http://en.wikipedia.org/wiki/Instrument_of_Accession_(Jammu_and_Kashmir)

http://www.jammu-kashmir.com/documents/jkunresolution.html

http://indiacode.nic.in/coiweb/amend/amend42.htm

http://en.wikipedia.org/wiki/Two-nation_theory

http://en.wikipedia.org/wiki/Article_370

http://www.time.com/time/interactive/0,31813,2025174,00.html

http://www.yojana.gov.in/topstory_details.asp?storyid=228 http://www.safhr.org/index.php?option=com_content&view=article&id=72:kashmir-chronology-of-key-events&catid=60:chronology-of-events&Itemid=358

http://www.bbc.co.uk/news/world-south-asia-16069078

http://www.greaterkashmir.com/news/2013/Feb/10/timeline-of-events-since-2001-parliament-attack-39.asp

## *Organizations/Institutions*

Women in Security, Conflict Management and Peace (WISCOMP), New Delhi

Institute for Conflict Management (ICM), New Delhi

Rajaratnam School of International Studies (RSIS), Singapore

Jagori, New Delhi

Centre for Dialogue and Reconciliation (CDR), New Delhi
Conciliation Resources (CR), London
Association of Parents of Disappeared Persons (APDP), Srinagar
Panos London, and Panos South Asia
London School of Economics and Political Science, London
Aman Biradari, New Delhi
The Other Media, New Delhi
Samarpan Foundation

# Notes

1 Hoskote, Ranjit (trans.); *I, Lalla: The Poems of Lal Ded*; Penguin (2011); Poem 90, Pg. 92

2 For a study of the extraordinary political status of the Northern Areas, see Ajai Sahni and Saji Cherian, 'Gilgit-Baltistan: The Laws of Occupation', *Faultlines: Writings on Conflict & Resolution*; Vol. 18; January 2007

3 *Ibid*

4 Akbar, M. J.; *Kashmir: Behind the Vale;* Roli Books (2002); Pg. 9

5 *Ibid*; Pg. x

6 Hoskote, Ranjit (trans.); *I, Lalla: The Poems of Lal Ded*; Penguin (2011); Poem 92, Pg. 94

7 *Ibid*; Poem 93, Pg. 95

8 *Ibid*; Pg. ix

9 *Ibid*; Poem 146, Pg. 148

10 Akbar, M.J.; *Kashmir: Behind The Vale*; Roli Books (2002); Pg 221

11 Although Sufis from Iran and Central Asia laid the foundations of Islam in Kashmir, it was an indigenous mystical order, the Muslim Rishis, which was actually instrumental in the spread of Islam in the region. Founded by Hazrat Nuruddin Nurani (1356–1440 CE), the Rishi order was particularly active from the fourteenth to the seventeenth century CE. Although the

Rishis were Muslims and saw the spread of Islam as their primary task, their message of love and tolerance transcending barriers of caste and creed endeared them to people of all communities. Bitterly critiquing social inequalities and superstitions as well as political oppression, they championed the cause of the poor and the marginalised. This is why the Rishis are still looked upon with great regard by all Kashmiris, Muslims, Hindus, Sikhs, as well as others.
http://www.svabhinava.org/abhinava/YoginderSikand/MuslimRishis-frame.php

12 Chadha Behera, Navnita; *Demystifying Kashmir;* The Brookings Institution (2006); Pg. 5

13 Akbar, M. J.; *Kashmir: Behind the Vale*; Roli Books (2002); Pg. vii

14 Rao, B.N.; in a speech made to the Security Council in February 1950

15 Gupta, S.; *Kashmir: A Study in India Pakistan Relations;* Asia Publishing House, 1996

16 Chadha Behera, Navnita; *Demystifying Kashmir;* The Brookings Institution (2006); Pg. 22

17 Anand, Justice A. S.; *Development of the Constitution of Jammu and Kashmir*; Light and Life (1980); Pg. 112-43

18 The Instrument of Accession is a legal document executed by Maharaja Hari Singh, ruler of the princely state of Jammu and Kashmir, on 26 October 1947. By executing this document under the provisions of the Indian Independence Act 1947, Maharaja Hari Singh agreed to accede to the Dominion of India.
http://en.wikipedia.org/wiki/Instrument_of_Accession_(Jammu_and_Kashmir)

19 For details on this, see Lamb, Alistair; *Kashmir: A Disputed Legacy 1846-1990*; Roxford Books (1991); Pg. 136-7

20 UN Resolution on Jammu and Kashmir, 1948
http://www.jammu-kashmir.com/documents/jkunresolution.html

21 http://indiacode.nic.in/coiweb/amend/amend42.htm

22 The Two-Nation theory is the ideology that the primary identity of Muslims on the Indian subcontinent is their religion, rather than their language or ethnicity, and therefore Indian Hindus and Muslims are two distinct nationalities, regardless of ethnic or other commonalities. The Two-Nation theory was a founding principle of the Pakistan Movement (i.e. the ideology of Pakistan as a Muslim nation-state in South Asia), and the Partition in 1947.
http://en.wikipedia.org/wiki/Two-nation_theory

23 Evans, Alexander; 'Reducing Tensions is not Enough'; *Washington Quarterly* 24, No. 2; (Spring 2001)

24 http://en.wikipedia.org/wiki/Article_370

25 Some text in this section has been taken from my paper 'Jammu and Kashmir: Women's Role in the post-1989 Insurgency' published in *Faultlines: Writings on Conflict & Resolution;* Vol. 19; April 2008

26 http://www.yojana.gov.in/topstory_details.asp?storyid=228

27 http://www.tehelka.com/do-women-enjoy-equal-rights-in-jk/

28 Wani, Arif Shafi Wani, *Greater Kashmir,* 27 November 2006

29 Pukhraj, Malika; *Song Sung True: A Memoir;* Kali for Women (2003)

30 Kersten, Holger; *Jesus Lived in India: His Unknown Life Before and After the Crucifixion*; Element (1994); Pg. 8

31 Koul, Sudha; *The Tiger Ladies: A Memoir of Kashmir*; Review (2002); Pg. 19

32 While authorities estimate the missing to number approximately 4,000, the Association of Disappeared Persons (APDP) estimates

there are actually between 8,000 and 10,000 missing people in the region. The number of publicly announced and reported half-widows in the Kashmir valley is between 2,000 and 2,500. Along with the plight of 6,000 orphans, the children of half-widows who are affected deeply by the conflict, this issue adds much to the crisis. True data and numbers for both half-orphans and half-widows are thought to be much higher.
http://www.guardian.co.uk/global-development/2010/oct/11/1

33 Banerjee, S.; 'Midsummer Madness over Human Rights'; *Economic and Political Weekly of India*; June 1990

34 Behera, N.C.; 'J&K: Making and Unmaking Identities'; *Himal*; November/ December 1996; Vol. 9, No. 8

35 Hoskote, Ranjit (trans.); *I, Lalla: The Poems of Lal Ded*; Penguin (2011); Poem 19, Pg. 21

36 Ibid; Poem 111, Pg. 113

37 http://freepresskashmir.com/kashmirs-half-widows-seethe-in-bloody-conflict-061114/

38 http://www.epw.in/civil-liberties/human-rights-kashmir.html

39 Hoskote, Ranjit (tranltd.); *I, Lalla: The Poems of Lal Ded*; Penguin (2011); Poem 142, Pg. 144

40 Norberg-Hodge, Helena; *Ancient Futures: Learning from Ladakh*; Sierra Club Books (1991)

41 Some text in this section has been taken from my article 'After the Cloudburst' published in *Himal* (March 2011)

42 Hoskote, Ranjit (trans.); *I, Lalla: The Poems of Lal Ded*; Penguin (2011); Poem 11, Pg. 13

43 *The Tribune*, '22 Hindus massacred in Doda', 6 May 2006

44 Kak, Sanjay (edited.); *Until My Freedom Has Come: The New Intafada In Kashmir*; 'Kashmir: A Place of Blood and Memory', Nitasha Kaul; Penguin (2011); Pg. 207-08

45 *Ibid*; 'Kashmiri Marginalities: Construction, Nature and Response', Gowhar Fazili; Pg. 223

46 Hoskote, Ranjit (trans.); *I, Lalla: The Poems of Lal Ded*; Penguin (2011); Poem 128, Pg. 130

47 Kak, Sanjay (edited); *Until My Freedom Has Come: The New Intifada in Kashmir*; 'Kashmir: A Place of Blood and Memory', Nitasha Kaul; Penguin (2011); Pg. 198

48 Austin, Alex, Martina Fischer & Norbert Ropers (edited); *Transforming Ethnopolitical Conflict: The Berghof Handbook*; VS-Verlag (2004); Pg. 60

49 Kak, Sanjay (edited); *Until My Freedom Has Come: The New Intifada in Kashmir*; 'Kashmir: A Time for Freedom', Angana Chatterji; Penguin (2011); Pg. 132

50 Akbar, M. J.; *Kashmir: Behind the Vale*; Roli Books (2002); Pg. 7

51 Hoskote, Ranjit (trans.); *I, Lalla: The Poems of Lal Ded*; Penguin (2011); Poem 25, Pg. 27

# Copyright Acknowledgements

Excerpts from *I, Lalla: The Poems of Lal Ded*, translated by Ranjit Hoskote (New Delhi: Penguin Books India, 2011), reproduced with permission from the publisher.

Excerpts from *Kashmir: Behind the Vale* by M.J. Akbar (New Delhi: Roli Books, 2002), reproduced with permission from the author.

Excerpts from *Until My Freedom Has Come: The New Intifada in Kashmir*, edited by Sanjay Kak (New Delhi: Penguin Books India, 2011), reproduced with permission from individual authors and the publisher.